RIDERS OF THE DAWN

Center Point
Large Print

Also by Max Brand® and available from
Center Point Large Print:

Melody and Cordoba
The Winged Horse
The Cure of Silver Cañon
The Red Well
Son of an Outlaw
Lightning of Gold
Daring Duval

RIDERS OF THE DAWN

A WESTERN DUO

Louis L'Amour

CENTER POINT LARGE PRINT
THORNDIKE, MAINE

This Circle Ⓥ Western is published by
Center Point Large Print in the year 2018 in
co-operation with Golden West Literary Agency.

First Edition
March 2018

Printed in the United States of America
on permanent paper.
Set in 16-point Times New Roman type.

ISBN: 978-1-68324-725-8

Library of Congress Cataloging-in-Publication Data

Names: L'Amour, Louis, 1908-1988, author. | L'Amour, Louis,
  1908-1988. Ride, you tonto riders. | L'Amour, Louis, 1908-1988.
  Riders of the dawn.
Title: Riders of the dawn : a western duo / Louis L'Amour.
Description: First Edition. | Thorndike, Maine : Center Point Large Print,
  2018. | Series: A Circle V western | Series: Center Point Large Print
  edition western
Identifiers: LCCN 2017056246 | ISBN 9781683247258
  (hardcover : alk. paper)
Subjects: LCSH: Large type books. | GSAFD: Western stories.
Classification: LCC PS3523.A446 A6 2018 | DDC 813/.52—dc23
LC record available at https://lccn.loc.gov/2017056246

TABLE OF CONTENTS

Ride, You Tonto Riders 15

Riders of the Dawn 87

INTRODUCTION

Louis Dearborn LaMoore (1908-1988) was born in Jamestown, North Dakota. He left home at fifteen and subsequently held a wide variety of jobs although he worked mostly as a merchant seaman. From his earliest youth, L'Amour had a love of verse. His first published work was a poem, "The Chap Worth While", appearing when he was eighteen years old in his former hometown's newspaper, the *Jamestown Sun*. It is the only poem from his early years that he left out of *Smoke from This Altar* which appeared in 1939 from Lusk Publishers in Oklahoma City, a book which L'Amour published himself; however, this poem is reproduced in *The Louis L'Amour Companion* (Andrews and McMeel, 1992) edited by Robert Weinberg. L'Amour wrote poems and articles for a number of small circulation arts magazines all through the early 1930s and, after hundreds of rejection slips, finally had his first story accepted, "Anything for a Pal" in *True Gang Life* (10/35). He returned in 1938 to live with his family where they had settled in Choctaw, Oklahoma, determined to make writing his career. He wrote a fight story bought by Standard Magazines that year and became acquainted with editor Leo Margulies who was to play an important rôle later in L'Amour's life. "The Town No Guns Could Tame" in *New Western* (3/40) was his first published Western story.

During the Second World War L'Amour was drafted and ultimately served with the U.S. Army Transportation Corps in Europe. However, in the two years before he was shipped out, he managed to write a great many adventure stories for Standard Magazines. The first story he published in 1946, the year of his discharge, was a Western, "Law of the Desert Born" in *Dime Western* (4/46). A call to Leo Margulies resulted in L'Amour's agreeing to write Western stories for the various Western pulp magazines published by Standard Magazines, a third of which appeared under the byline Jim Mayo, the name of a character in L'Amour's earlier adventure fiction. The proposal for L'Amour to write new Hopalong Cassidy novels came from Margulies who wanted to launch *Hopalong Cassidy's Western Magazine* to take advantage of the popularity William Boyd's old films and new television series were enjoying with a new generation. Doubleday & Company agreed to publish the pulp novelettes in hardcover books. L'Amour was paid $500 a story, no royalties, and he was assigned the house name Tex Burns. L'Amour read Clarence E. Mulford's books about the Bar-20 and based his Hopalong Cassidy on Mulford's original creation. Only two issues of the magazine appeared before it ceased publication. Doubleday felt that the Hopalong character had to appear exactly as William Boyd did in the films and on television and thus even the first two novels had to be revamped to meet with this requirement prior to publication in book form.

L'Amour's first Western novel under his own byline was *Westward the Tide* (World's Work, 1950). It was rejected by every American publisher to which it was submitted. World's Work paid a flat £75 without royalties for British Empire rights in perpetuity. L'Amour sold his first Western short story to a slick magazine a year later, "The Gift of Cochise" in *Collier's* (7/5/52). Robert Fellows and John Wayne purchased screen rights to this story from L'Amour for $4,000 and James Edward Grant, one of Wayne's favorite screenwriters, developed a script from it, changing L'Amour's Ches Lane to Hondo Lane. L'Amour retained the right to novelize Grant's screenplay, which differs substantially from his short story, and he was able to get an endorsement from Wayne to be used as a blurb, stating that *Hondo* was the finest Western Wayne had ever read. *Hondo* (Fawcett Gold Medal, 1953) by Louis L'Amour was released on the same day as the film, *Hondo* (Warner, 1953), with a first printing of 320,000 copies.

With *Showdown at Yellow Butte* (Ace, 1953) by Jim Mayo, L'Amour began a series of short Western novels for Don Wollheim that could be doubled with other short novels by other authors in Ace Publishing's paperback two-fers. Advances on these were $800 and usually the author never earned any royalties. *Heller with a Gun* (Fawcett Gold Medal, 1955) was the first of a series of original Westerns L'Amour had agreed to write under his own name following the success for Fawcett of *Hondo*. Already this early L'Amour wanted to have his Western novels published in hard-cover editions. He expanded "Guns of the Timberland" by Jim Mayo in *West* (9/50) for *Guns of the Timberlands* (Jason Press, 1955), a hard-cover Western for which he was paid an advance of $250. Another novel for Jason Press followed and then *Silver Cañon* (Avalon Books, 1956) for Thomas Bouregy & Company. These were basically lending library publishers and the books seldom earned much money above the small advances paid.

The great turn in L'Amour's fortunes came about because of problems Saul David was having with his original paperback Westerns program at Bantam Books. Fred Glidden had been signed to a contract to produce two original paperback Western novels a year under the pseudonym Luke Short for an advance of $15,000 each. It was a long-term contract but, in the first ten years of it, Fred only wrote six novels. Literary agent Marguerite Harper then persuaded Bantam that Fred's brother, Jon, could help fulfill the contract and Jon was signed for eight Western novels under the pseudonym Peter Dawson. When Jon died suddenly before completing even one book for Bantam, Harper managed to engage a ghost writer at the Disney studios to write these eight "Peter Dawson" novels, beginning with *The Savages* (Bantam, 1959). They proved inferior to anything Jon had ever written and what sales they had seemed to be due only to the Peter Dawson name.

Saul David wanted to know from L'Amour if *he* could deliver two Western novels a year. L'Amour said he could, and he did. In fact, by 1962 this number was increased to three original paperback novels a year. The first L'Amour novel to appear under the Bantam contract was *Radigan* (Bantam, 1958).

The marketing strategy used to promote L'Amour was to keep *all* of his Western titles in print. Independent distributors were required to buy titles in lots of 10,000 copies if they wanted access to other Bantam titles at significantly discounted prices. In time L'Amour's paperbacks forced almost everyone else off the racks in the Western sections. L'Amour himself comprised the other half of this successful strategy. Dressed in Western attire, he traveled about the country in a motor home visiting with independent distributors, taking them to dinner and charming them, making them personal friends. He promoted himself at every available opportunity. L'Amour insisted that he was telling the stories of the people who had made America a great nation and he appealed to patriotism as much as to commercialism in his rhetoric.

His fiction suffered, of course; stories written hurriedly and submitted in their first draft and published as he wrote them. A character would have a rifle in his hand, a model not yet invented in the period in which the story was set, and when he crossed a street the rifle would vanish without explanation. A scene would begin in a saloon and suddenly the setting would be a hotel dining room. Characters would die once and, a few pages later, die again. An old man for most of a story would turn out to be in his twenties.

All of this notwithstanding, there are many fine, and some spectacular, moments in Louis L'Amour's Western fiction. Much of his early fiction possesses several of the characteristics in purest form which, no matter how diluted they ultimately would become, account in largest measure for the loyal following Louis L'Amour won from his readers: the young male narrator who is in the process of growing into manhood and who is evaluating other human beings and his own experiences; a resourceful frontier woman who has beauty as well as fortitude; a strong male character who is single and hence marriageable; and the powerful, romantic, strangely compelling vision of the American West which invests L'Amour's Western fiction and makes it such a delightful escape from the cares of a later time—in the author's own words from one of his stories, that "big country needing big men and women to live in it" and where there was no place for "the frightened or the mean."

RIDE, YOU
TONTO RIDERS

I

The rain, which had been falling steadily for three days, had turned the trail into a sloppy river of mud. Peering through the slanting downpour, Mathurin Sabre cursed himself for the quixotic notion that impelled him to take this special trail to the home of the man that he had gunned down.

Nothing good could come of it, he reflected, yet the thought that the young widow and child might need the money he was carrying had started him upon the long ride from El Paso to the Mogollons. Certainly neither the bartender nor the hangers-on in the saloon could have been entrusted with that money, and nobody was taking that dangerous ride to the Tonto Basin for fun.

Matt Sabre was no trouble hunter. At various times, he had been many things, most of them associated with violence. By birth and inclination, he was a Western man, although much of his adult life had been lived far from his native country. He had been a buffalo hunter, a prospector, and for a short time a two-gun marshal of a tough cattle town. It was his stubborn refusal either to back up or back down that kept him in constant hot water.

Yet some of his trouble derived from something

17

more than that. It stemmed from a dark and bitter drive toward violence—a drive that lay deeply within him. He was aware of this drive and held it in restraint, but at times it welled up, and he went smashing into trouble—a big, rugged, and dangerous man who fought like a Viking gone berserk, except that he fought coldly and shrewdly.

He was a tall man, heavier than he appeared, and his lean, dark face had a slightly patrician look with high cheek bones and green eyes. His eyes were usually quiet and reserved. He had a natural affinity for horses and weapons. He understood them, and they understood him. It had been love of a good horse that brought him to his first act of violence.

He had been buffalo hunting with his uncle and had interfered with another hunter who was beating his horse. At sixteen, a buffalo hunter was a man and expected to stand as one. Matt Sabre stood his ground and shot it out, killing his first man. Had it rested there, all would have been well, but two of the dead man's friends had come hunting Sabre. Failing to find him, they had beaten his ailing uncle and stolen the horses. Matt Sabre trailed them to Mobeetie and killed them both in the street, taking his horses home.

Then he left the country, to prospect in Mexico, fight a revolution in Central America, and join the Foreign Legion in Morocco, from which he deserted after two years. Returning to Texas, he drove a trail herd up to Dodge, then took a job as marshal of a town. Six months later, in El Paso, he had become engaged in an altercation with Billy Curtin, and Curtin had called him a liar and gone for his gun.

With that incredible speed that was so much a part of him, Matt drew his gun and fired. Curtin hit the floor. An hour later, he was summoned to the dying man's hotel room.

Billy Curtin, his dark, tumbled hair against a folded blanket, his face drawn and deathly white, was dying. They told him outside the door that Curtin might live an hour or even two. He could not live longer.

Tall, straight, and quiet, Sabre walked into the room and stood by the dying man's bed. Curtin held a packet wrapped in oilskin. "Five thousand dollars," he whispered. "Take it to my wife . . . to Jenny, on the Pivotrock, in the Mogollons. She's in . . . in . . . trouble."

It was a curious thing that this dying man should place a trust in the hands of the man who had killed him. Sabre stared down at him, frowning a little.

"Why me?" he asked. "You trust me with this? And why should I do it?"

"You . . . you're a gentleman. I trust you to help her. Will you? I . . . I was a hot-headed fool. Worried . . . impatient. It wasn't your fault."

The reckless light was gone from the blue eyes, and the light that remained was fading.

"I'll do it, Curtin. You've my word . . . you've got the word of Matt Sabre."

For an instant, then, the blue eyes blazed widely and sharply with knowledge. "You're . . . Sabre?"

Matt nodded, but the light had faded, and Billy Curtin had bunched his herd.

It had been a rough and bitter trip, but there was a little farther to go. West of El Paso there had been a brush with marauding Apaches. In Silver City, two strangely familiar riders had followed him into a saloon and started a brawl. Yet Matt was too wise in the ways of thieves to be caught by so obvious a trick, and he had slipped away in the darkness after shooting out the light.

The roan slipped now on the muddy trail, scrambled up, and moved on through the trees. Suddenly, in the rain-darkened dusk, there was one light, then another.

"Yellow Jacket," Matt said with a sigh of relief. "That means a good bed for us, boy. A good bed and a good feed."

Yellow Jacket was a jumping-off place. It was a stage station and a saloon, a livery stable and a ramshackle hotel. It was a cluster of adobe residences and some false-fronted stores. It bunched its buildings in a corner of Copper Creek.

It was Galusha Reed's town, and Reed owned the Yellow Jacket Saloon and the Rincon Mine. Sid Trumbull was town marshal, and he ran the place for Reed. Wherever Reed rode, Tony Sikes was close by, and there were some who said that Reed in turn was owned by Prince McCarran, who owned the big PM brand in the Tonto Basin country.

Matt Sabre stabled his horse and turned to the slope-shouldered liveryman. "Give him a bait of corn. Another in the morning."

"Corn?" Simpson shook his head. "We've no corn."

"You have corn for the freighters' stock and corn for the stage horses. Give my horse corn."

Sabre had a sharp ring of authority in his voice, and, before he realized it, Simpson was giving the big roan his corn. He thought about it and stared after Sabre. The tall rider was walking away, a light, long step, easy and free, on the balls of his feet. And he carried two guns, low-hung and tied-down.

Simpson stared, then shrugged. "A bad one," he muttered. "Wish he'd kill Sid Trumbull."

Matt Sabre pushed into the door of the Yellow Jacket and dropped his saddlebags to the floor. Then he strode to the bar. "What have you got, man? Anything but rye?"

"What's the matter? Ain't rye good enough for

21

you?" The bartender, a man named Hobbs, was sore himself. No man should work so many hours on feet like his.

"Have you brandy? Or some Irish whiskey?"

Hobbs stared. "Mister, where do you think you are? New York?"

"That's all right, Hobbs. I like a man who knows what he likes. Give him some of my cognac."

Matt Sabre turned and glanced at the speaker. He was a tall man, immaculate in black broadcloth, with blond hair slightly wavy and a rosy complexion. He might have been thirty or older. He wore a pistol on his left side, high up.

"Thanks," Sabre said briefly. "There's nothing better than cognac on a wet night."

"My name is McCarran. I run the PM outfit, east of here. Northeast, to be exact."

Sabre nodded. "My name is Sabre. I run no outfit, but I'm looking for one. Where's the Pivotrock?"

He was a good poker player, men said. His eyes were fast from using guns, and so he saw the sudden glint and the quick caution in Prince McCarran's eyes.

"The Pivotrock? Why, that's a stream over in the Mogollons. There's an outfit over there, all right. A one-horse affair. Why do you ask?"

Sabre cut him off short. "Business with them."

"I see. Well, you'll find it a lonely ride. There's

22

trouble up that way now, some sort of a cattle war."

Matt Sabre tasted his drink. It was good cognac. In fact, it was the best, and he had found none west of New Orleans.

McCarran, his name was. He knew something, too. Curtin had asked him to help his widow. Was the Pivotrock outfit in the war? He decided against asking McCarran, and they talked quietly of the rain and of cattle, then of cognac. "You never acquired a taste for cognac in the West. May I ask where?"

"Paris," Sabre replied, "Marseilles, Fez, and Marrakesh."

"You've been around, then. Well, that's not uncommon." The blond man pointed toward a heavy-shouldered young man who slept with his head on his arms. "See that chap? Calls himself Camp Gordon. He's a Cambridge man, quotes the classics when he's drunk . . . which is over half the time . . . and is one of the best cowhands in the country when he's sober. Keys over there, playing the piano, studied in Weimar. He knew Strauss, in Vienna, before he wrote 'The Blue Danube'. There's all sorts of men in the West, from belted earls and remittance men to vagabond scum from all corners of the world. They are here a few weeks, and they talk the lingo like veterans. Some of the biggest ranches in the West are owned by Englishmen."

Prince McCarran talked to him a few minutes longer, but he learned nothing. Sabre was not evasive, but somehow he gave out no information about himself or his mission. McCarran walked away very thoughtfully. Later, after Matt Sabre was gone, Sid Trumbull came in.

"Sabre?" Trumbull shook his head. "Never heard of him. Keys might know. He knows about ever'body. What's he want on the Pivotrock?"

Lying on his back in bed, Matt Sabre stared up into the darkness and listened to the rain on the window and on the roof. It rattled hard, skeleton fingers against the glass, and he turned restlessly in his bed, frowning as he recalled that quick, guarded expression in the eyes of Prince McCarran.

Who was McCarran, and what did he know? Had Curtin's request that he help his wife been merely the natural request of a dying man, or had he felt that there was a definite need of help? Was something wrong here?

He went to sleep vowing to deliver the money and ride away. Yet even as his eyes closed the last time, he knew he would not do it if there was trouble.

It was still raining, but no longer pouring, when he awakened. He dressed swiftly and checked his guns, his mind taking up his problems where they had been left the previous night.

Camp Gordon, his face puffy from too much drinking and too sound asleep, staggered down the stairs after him. He grinned woefully at Sabre. "I guess I really hung one on last night," he said. "What I need is to get out of town."

They ate breakfast together, and Gordon's eyes sharpened suddenly at Matt's query of directions to the Pivotrock. "You'll not want to go there, man. Since Curtin ran out, they've got their backs to the wall. They are through! Leave it to Galusha Reed for that."

"What's the trouble?"

"Reed claims title to the Pivotrock. Bill Curtin's old man bought it from a Mex who had it from a land grant. Then he made a deal with the Apaches, which seemed to cinch his title. Trouble was, Galusha Reed shows up with a prior claim. He says Fernandez had no grant. That his man Sonoma had a prior one. Old Man Curtin was killed when he fell from his buckboard, and young Billy couldn't stand the gaff. He blew town after Tony Sikes buffaloed him."

"What about his wife?"

Gordon shook his head, then shrugged. Doubt and worry struggled on his face. "She's a fine girl, Jenny Curtin is. The salt of the earth. It's too bad Curtin hadn't a tenth of her nerve. She'll stick, and she swears she'll fight."

"Has she any men?"

"Two. An old man who was with her father-in-law and a half-breed Apache they call Rado. It used to be Silverado."

Thinking it over, Sabre decided there was much left to be explained. Where had the $5,000 come from? Had Billy really run out, or had he gone away to get money to put up a battle? And how did he get it?

"I'm going out." Sabre got to his feet. "I'll have a talk with her."

"Don't take a job there. She hasn't a chance," Gordon said grimly. "You'd do well to stay away."

"I like fights when one side doesn't have a chance," Matt replied lightly. "Maybe I will ask for a job. A man's got to die sometime, and what better time than fighting when the odds are against him?"

"I like to win," Gordon said flatly. "I like at least a chance."

Matt Sabre leaned over the table, aware that Prince McCarran had moved up behind Gordon, and that a big man with a star was standing near him. "If I decide to go to work for her"—Sabre's voice was easy, confident—"then you'd better join us. Our side will win."

"Look here, you!" The man wearing the star, Sid Trumbull, stepped forward. "You either stay in town or get down the trail! There's trouble enough in the Mogollons. Stay out of there."

Matt looked up. "You're telling me?" His voice

cracked like a whip. "You're town marshal, Trumbull, not a United States marshal or a sheriff, and, if you were a sheriff, it wouldn't matter. It is out of this county. Now suppose you back up and don't step into conversations unless you're invited."

Trumbull's head lowered, and his face flushed red. Then he stepped around the table, his eyes narrow and mean. "Listen, you!" His voice was thick with fury. "No two-by-twice cowpoke tells me . . . !"

"Trumbull"—Sabre spoke evenly—"you're asking for it. You aren't acting in the line of duty now. You're picking trouble, and the fact that you're marshal won't protect you."

"Protect me?" His fury exploded. "Protect me? Why, you . . . !"

Trumbull lunged around the table, but Matt side-stepped swiftly and kicked a chair into the marshal's path. Enraged, Sid Trumbull had no chance to avoid it and fell headlong, bloodying his palms on the slivery floor.

Kicking the chair away, he lunged to his feet, and Matt stood facing him, smiling. Camp Gordon was grinning, and Hobbs was leaning his forearms on the bar, watching with relish.

Trumbull stared at his torn palms, then lifted his eyes to Sabre's. Then he started forward, and suddenly, in mid-stride, his hand swept for his gun.

Sabre palmed his Colt, and the gun barked even as it lifted. Stunned, Sid Trumbull stared at his numbed hand. His gun had been knocked spinning, and the .44 slug, hitting the trigger guard, had gone by to rip off the end of Sid's little finger. Dumbly he stared at the slow drip of blood.

Prince McCarran and Gordon were only two of those who stared, not at the marshal, but at Matt Sabre.

"You throw that gun mighty fast, stranger," McCarran said. "Who are you, anyway? There aren't a half dozen men in the country who can throw a gun that fast. I know most of them by sight."

Sabre's eyes glinted coldly. "No? Well, you know another one now. Call it seven men." He spun on his heel and strode from the room. All eyes followed him.

II

Matt Sabre's roan headed up Shirt Tail Creek, crossed Bloody Basin and Skeleton Ridge, and made the Verde in the vicinity of the hot springs. He bedded down that night in a corner of a cliff near Hardscrabble Creek. It was late when he turned in, and he had lit no fire.

He had chosen his position well, for behind him

28

the cliff towered, and on his left there was a steep hillside that sloped away toward Hardscrabble Creek. He was almost at the foot of Hardscrabble Mesa, with the rising ground of Deadman Mesa before him. The ground in front sloped away to the creek, and there was plenty of dry wood. The overhang of the cliff protected it from the rain.

Matt Sabre came suddenly awake. For an instant, he lay very still. The sky had cleared, and, as he lay on his side, he could see the stars. He judged that it was past midnight. Why he had awakened he could not guess, but he saw that the roan was nearer, and the big gelding had his head up and ears pricked.

"Careful, boy," Sabre warned.

Sliding out of his bedroll, he drew on his boots and got to his feet. Feeling out in the darkness, he drew his Winchester near.

He was sitting in absolute blackness due to the cliff's overhang. He knew the boulders and the clumps of cedar were added concealment. The roan would be lost against the blackness of the cliff, but from where he sat, he could see some thirty yards of the creekbank and some open ground.

There was subdued movement below and whispering voices. Then silence. Leaving his rifle, Sabre belted on his guns and slid quietly out of the overhang and into the cedars.

After a moment, he heard the sound of movement, and then a low voice: "He can't be far. They said he came this way, and he left the main trail after Fossil Creek."

There were two of them. He waited, standing there among the cedars, his eyes hard and his muscles poised and ready. They were fools. Did they think he was that easy?

He had fought Apaches and Kiowas, and he had fought the Tauregs in the Sahara and the Riffs in the Atlas Mountains. He saw them then, saw their dark figures moving up the hill, outlined against the pale gravel of the slope.

That hard, bitter thing inside him broke loose, and he could not stand still. He could not wait. They would find the roan, and then they would not leave until they had him. It was now or never. He stepped out quickly, silently.

"Looking for somebody?"

They wheeled, and he saw the starlight on a pistol barrel and heard the flat, husky cough of his own gun. One went down, gasping. The other staggered, then turned and started off in a stumbling run, moaning half in fright, half in pain. He stood there, trying to follow the man, but he lost him in the brush.

He turned back to the fellow on the ground but did not go near him. He circled widely instead, returning to his horse. He quieted his roan, then lay down. In a few minutes, he was dozing.

Daybreak found him standing over the body. The roan was already saddled for the trail. It was one of the two he had seen in Silver City, a lean, dark-faced man with deep lines in his cheeks and a few gray hairs at the temples. There was an old scar, deep and red, over his eye.

Sabre knelt and went through his pockets, taking a few letters and some papers. He stuffed them into his own pockets, then mounted. Riding warily, he started up the creek. He rode with his Winchester across his saddle, ready for whatever came. Nothing did.

The morning drew on, the air warm and still after the rain. A fly buzzed around his ears, and he whipped it away with his hat. The roan had a long-striding, space-eating walk. It moved out swiftly and surely toward the far purple ranges, dipping down through grassy meadows lined with pines and aspens, with here and there the whispering leaves of a tall cottonwood.

It was a land to dream about, a land perfect for the grazing of either cattle or sheep, a land for a man to live in. Ahead and on his left he could see the towering Mogollon Rim, and it was beyond this rim, up on the plateau, that he would find the Pivotrock. He skirted a grove of rustling aspen and looked down a long valley.

For the first time, he saw cattle—fat, contented cattle, fat from the rich grass of these bottom lands. Once, far off, he glimpsed a rider, but he made no effort to draw near, wanting only to find the trail to the Pivotrock.

A wide-mouthed cañon opened from the northeast, and he turned the roan and started up the creek that ran down it. Now he was climbing, and from the look of the country, he would climb nearly three thousand feet to reach the rim. Yet he had been told there was a trail ahead, and he pushed on.

The final eight hundred feet to the rim was by a switchback trail that had him climbing steadily, yet the air on the plateau atop the rim was amazingly fresh and clear. He pushed on, seeing a few scattered cattle, and then he saw a crude wooden sign by the narrow trail. It read: PIVOTROCK 1 MILE

The house was low and sprawling, lying on a flat-topped knoll with the long barns and sheds built on three sides of a square. The open side faced the rim and the trail up which he was riding. There were cottonwood, pine, and fir backing up the buildings. He could see the late afternoon sunlight glistening on the coats of the saddle stock in the corral.

An old man stepped from the stable with a carbine in his hands. "All right, stranger. You stop where you are. What you want here?"

Matt Sabre grinned. Lifting his hand carefully,

he pushed back his flat-brimmed hat. "Huntin' Missus Jenny Curtin," he said. "I've got news." He hesitated. "Of her husband."

The carbine muzzle lowered. "Of him? What news would there be of him?"

"Not good news," Sabre told him. "He's dead."

Surprisingly the old man seemed relieved. "Light," he said briefly. "I reckon we figured he was dead. How'd it happen?"

Sabre hesitated. "He picked a fight in a saloon in El Paso, then drew too slow."

"He was never fast." The old man studied him. "My name's Tom Judson. Now, you sure didn't come all the way here from El Paso to tell us Billy was dead. What did you come for?"

"I'll tell Missus Curtin that. However, they tell me down the road you've been with her a long time, so you might as well know. I brought her some money. Bill Curtin gave it to me on his deathbed, asked me to bring it to her. It's five thousand dollars."

"Five thousand?" Judson stared. "Reckon Bill must have set some store by you to trust you with it. Know him long?"

Sabre shook his head. "Only a few minutes. A dying man hasn't much choice."

A door slammed up at the house, and they both turned. A slender girl was walking toward them, and the sunlight caught the red in her hair. She wore a simple cotton dress, but her figure was

33

trim and neat. Ahead of her dashed a boy who might have been five or six. He lunged at Sabre, then slid to a stop, and stared up at him, then at his guns.

"Howdy, old-timer!" Sabre said, smiling. "Where's your spurs?"

The boy was startled and shy. He drew back, surprised at the question. "I . . . I've got no spurs!"

"What? A cowhand without spurs? We'll have to fix that." He looked up. "How are you, Missus Curtin? I'm Mathurin Sabre, Matt for short. I'm afraid I've some bad news for you."

Her face paled a little, but her chin lifted. "Will you come to the house, Mister . . . Sabre? Tom, put his horse in the corral, will you?"

The living room of the ranch house was spacious and cool. There were Navajo rugs upon the floor, and the chairs and the divan were beautifully tanned cowhide. He glanced around appreciatively, enjoying the coolness after his hot ride in the Arizona sun, like the naturalness of this girl, standing in the home she had created.

She faced him abruptly. "Perhaps you'd better tell me now. There's no use pretending or putting a bold face on it when I have to be told."

As quickly and quietly as possible, he explained. When he was finished, her face was white and still. "I . . . I was afraid of this. When he rode away, I knew he would never come back.

34

You see, he thought . . . he believed he had failed me, failed his father."

Matt drew the oilskin packet from his pocket. "He sent you this. He said it was five thousand dollars. He said to give it to you."

She took it, staring at the package, and tears welled into her eyes. "Yes." Her voice was so low that Matt scarcely heard it. "He would do this. He probably felt it was all he could do for me, for us. You see"—Jenny Curtin's eyes lifted—"we're in a fight, and a bad one. This is war money. I . . . guess Billy thought . . . well, he was no fighter himself, and this might help, might compensate. You're probably wondering about all this."

"No," he said. "I'm not. And maybe I'd better go out with the boys now. You'll want to be alone."

"Wait!" Her fingers caught his sleeve. "I want you to know, since you were with him when he died, and you have come all this way to help us. There was no trouble with Billy and me. It was . . . well, he thought he was a coward. He thought he had failed me. We've had trouble with Galusha Reed in Yellow Jacket. Tony Sikes picked a fight with Billy. He wanted to kill him, and Billy wouldn't fight. He . . . he backed down. Everybody said he was a coward, and he ran. He went . . . away."

Matt Sabre frowned thoughtfully, staring at the floor. The boy who picked a fight with him, who

35

dared him, who went for his gun, was no coward. Trying to prove something to himself? Maybe. But no coward.

"Ma'am," he said abruptly, "you're his widow. The mother of his child. There's something you should know. Whatever else he was, I don't know. I never knew him long enough. But that man was no coward. Not even a little bit. You see . . . ,"—Matt hesitated, feeling the falseness of his position, not wanting to tell this girl that he had killed her husband, yet not wanting her to think him a coward—"I saw his eyes when he went for his gun. I was there, ma'am, and saw it all. Bill Curtin was no coward."

Hours later, lying in his bunk, he thought of it, and the five thousand dollars was still a mystery. Where had it come from? How had Curtin come by it?

He turned over and after a few minutes went to sleep. The next day, he would be riding.

The sunlight was bright the next morning when he finally rolled out of bed. He bathed and shaved, taking his time, enjoying the sun on his back, and feeling glad he was footloose again. He was in the bunkhouse, belting on his guns, when he heard the horses. He stepped to the door and glanced out.

Neither the dark-faced Rado nor Judson was about, and there were three riders in the yard.

36

One of them he recognized as a man from Yellow Jacket, and the tallest of the riders was Galusha Reed. He was a big man, broad and thick in the body without being fat. His jaw was brutal.

Jenny Curtin came out on the steps.

"Ma'am," Reed said abruptly, "we're movin' you off this land. We're goin' to give you ten minutes to pack, an' one of my boys'll hitch the buckboard for you. This here trouble's gone on long enough, an' mine's the prior claim to this land. You're gettin' off."

Jenny's eyes turned quickly toward the stable, but Reed shook his head. "You needn't look for Judson or the 'breed. We watched until we seen them away from here, an' some of my boys are coverin' the trail. We're tryin' to get you off here without any trouble."

"You can turn around and leave, Mister Reed. I'm not going!"

"I reckon you are," Reed said patiently. "We know that your man's dead. We just can't put up with you squattin' on our range."

"This happens to be my range, and I'm staying."

Reed chuckled. "Don't make us put you off, ma'am. Don't make us get rough. Up here"—he waved a casual hand—"we can do anything we want, and nobody the wiser. You're leavin', as of now."

Matt Sabre stepped out of the bunkhouse and

took three quick steps toward the riders. He was cool and sure of himself, but he could feel the jumping invitation to trouble surging up inside him. He fought it down and held himself still for an instant. Then he spoke.

"Reed, you're a fat-headed fool and a bully. You ride up here to take advantage of a woman because you think she's helpless. Well, she's not. Now you three turn your horses . . . turn 'em mighty careful . . . and start down the trail. And don't you ever set foot on this place again."

Reed's face went white, then dark with anger. He leaned forward a little. "So you're still here? Well, we'll give you a chance to run. Get goin'!"

Matt Sabre walked forward another step. He could feel the eagerness pushing up inside him, and his eyes held the three men, and he saw the eyes of one widen with apprehension.

"Watch it, boss! Watch it!"

"That's right, Reed. Watch it. You figured to find this girl alone. Well, she's not alone. Furthermore, if she'll take me on as a hand, I'll stay. I'll stay until you're out of the country or dead. You can have it either way you want. There's three of you. I like that. That evens us up. If you want to feed buzzards, just edge that hand another half inch toward your gun and you can. That goes for the three of you."

He stepped forward again. He was jumping with it now—that old drive for combat welling up within him. Inside, he was trembling, but his muscles were steady, and his mind was cool and ready. His fingers spread, and he moved forward again.

"Come on, you mangy coyotes. Let's see if you've got the nerve. Reach!"

Reed's face was still and cold. His mouth looked pinched, and his eyes were wide. Some sixth sense warned him that this was different. This was death he was looking at, and Galusha Reed suddenly realized he was no gambler when the stakes were so high.

He could see the dark eagerness that was driving this cool man; he could see beyond the coolness on his surface the fierceness of his readiness; inside, he went sick and cold at the thought.

"Boss," the man at his side whispered hoarsely, "let's get out of here. This man's poison."

Galusha Reed slowly eased his hand forward to the pommel of the saddle. "So, Jenny, you're hiring gunfighters? Is that the way you want it?"

"I think you hired them first," she replied coolly. "Now you'd better go."

"On the way back," Sabre suggested, "you might stop in Hardscrabble Cañon and pick up the body of one of your killers. He guessed wrong last night."

Reed stared at him. "I don't know what you mean!" he flared. "I sent out no killer."

Matt Sabre watched the three men ride down the trail and he frowned. There had been honest doubt in Reed's eyes, but if he had not sent the two men after him, who had? Those men had been in Silver City and El Paso, yet they also knew this country and knew someone in Yellow Jacket. Maybe they had not come after him but had first followed Bill Curtin.

He turned and smiled at the girl. "Coyotes," he said, shrugging. "Not much heart in them."

She was staring at him strangely. "You . . . you'd have killed them, wouldn't you? Why?"

He shrugged. "I don't know. Maybe it's because . . . well, I don't like to see men take advantage of a woman alone. Anyway"—he smiled—"Reed doesn't impress me as a good citizen."

"He's a dangerous enemy." She came down from the steps. "Did you mean what you said, Mister Sabre? I mean, about staying here and working for me? I need men, although I must tell you that you've small chance of winning, and it's rather a lonely fight."

"Yes, I meant it." Did he mean it? Of course. He remembered the old Chinese proverb: If you save a person's life, he becomes your responsibility. That wasn't the case here, but he had killed this girl's husband, and the least he could do would be to stay until she was out of trouble. Was that all he was thinking of? "I'll stay," he said. "I'll see you through this. I've been fighting all my life, and it would be a shame to stop now. And I've fought for lots less reasons."

III

Throughout the morning, he worked around the place. He worked partly because there was much to be done and partly because he wanted to think.

The horses in the remuda were held on the home place and were in good shape. Also, they were better than the usual ranch horses, for some of them showed a strong Morgan strain. He repaired the latch on the stable door and walked around the place, sizing it up from every angle, studying all the approaches.

With his glasses, he studied the hills and searched the notches and cañons wherever he could see them. Mentally he formed a map of all that terrain within reach of his glass.

It was midafternoon before Judson and Rado returned, and they had talked with Jenny before he saw them.

"Howdy." Judson was friendly, but his eyes studied Sabre with care. "Miz Jenny tells me you run Reed off. That you're aimin' to stay on here."

"That's right. I'll stay until she's out of trouble,

41

if she'll have me. I don't like being pushed around."

"No, neither do I." Judson was silent for several moments, and then he turned his eyes on Sabre. "Don't you be gettin' any ideas about Miz Jenny. She's a fine girl."

Matt looked up angrily. "And don't you be getting any ideas," he said coldly. "I'm helping her the same as you are, and we'll work together. As to personal things, leave them alone. I'll only say that when this fight is over, I'm hitting the trail."

"All right," Judson said mildly. "We can use help."

Three days passed smoothly. Matt threw himself into the work of the ranch, and he worked feverishly. Even he could not have said why he worked so desperately hard. He dug post holes and fenced an area in the long meadow near the seeping springs in the bottom.

Then, working with Rado, he rounded up the cattle nearest the rim and pushed them back behind the fence. The grass was thick and deep there and would stand a lot of grazing, for the meadow wound back up the cañon for some distance. He carried a running iron and branded stock wherever he found it required.

As the ranch had been short-handed for a year, there was much to do. Evenings, he mended gear and worked around the place, and at night he slept soundly. During all this time, he saw nothing of Jenny Curtin.

He saw nothing of her, but she was constantly in his thoughts. He remembered her as he had seen her that first time, standing in the living room of the house, listening to him, her eyes, wide and dark, upon his face. He remembered her facing Galusha Reed and his riders from the steps.

Was he staying on because he believed he owed her a debt or because of her?

Here and there around the ranch, Sabre found small, intangible hints of the sort of man Curtin must have been. Judson had liked him, and so had the half-breed. He had been gentle with horses. He had been thoughtful. Yet he had hated and avoided violence. Slowly, rightly or wrongly Matt could not tell, a picture was forming in his mind of a fine young man who had been totally out of place.

Western birth, but born for peaceful and quiet ways, he had been thrown into a cattle war and had been aware of his own inadequacy. Matt was thinking of that, and working at a rawhide reata, when Jenny came up.

He had not seen her approach, or he might have avoided her, but she was there beside him before he realized it.

"You're working hard, Mister Sabre."

"To earn my keep, ma'am. There's a lot to do, I find, and I like to keep busy." He turned the reata and studied it. "You know, there's something I've been wanting to talk to you about. Maybe it's none of my affair, but young Billy is going to grow up, and he's going to ask questions about his dad. You aren't going to be able to fool him. Maybe you know what this is all about, and maybe I'm mounting on the offside, but it seems to me that Bill Curtin went to El Paso to get that money for you.

"I think he realized he was no fighting man, and that the best thing he could do was to get that money so he could hire gunfighters. It took nerve to do what he did, and I think he deliberately took what Sikes handed him because he knew that, if Sikes killed him, you'd never get that money.

"Maybe along the way to El Paso he began to wonder, and maybe he picked that fight down there with the idea of proving to himself that he did have the nerve to face a gun."

She did not reply, but stood there, watching his fingers work swiftly and evenly, plaiting the leather.

"Yes," she said finally, "I thought of that. Only I can't imagine where he got the money. I hesitate to use it without knowing."

"Don't be foolish," he said irritably. "Use it. Nobody would put it to better use, and you need gun hands."

"But who would work for me?" Her voice was low and bitter. "Galusha Reed has seen to it that no one will."

"Maybe if I rode in, I could find some men." He was thinking of Camp Gordon, the Shakespeare-quoting English cowhand. "I believe I know one man."

"There's a lot to be done. Jud tells me you've been doing the work of three men."

Matt Sabre got to his feet. She stepped back a little, suddenly aware of how tall he was. She was tall for a girl, yet she came no farther than his lips. She drew back a little at the thought. Her eyes dropped to his guns. He always wore them, always low and tied-down.

"Judson said you were a fast man with a gun. He said you had the mark of the . . . of the gunfighter."

"Probably." He found no bitterness at the thought. "I've used guns. Guns and horses, they are about all I've known."

"Where were you in the army? I've watched you walk and ride and you show military training."

"Oh, several places. Africa mostly."

"Africa?" She was amazed. "You've been there?"

He nodded. "Desert and mountain country. Morocco and the Sahara, all the way to Timbuktu and Lake Chad, fighting most of the time."

45

It was growing dark in the shed where they were standing. He moved out into the dusk. A few stars had already appeared, and the red glow that was in the west beyond the rim was fading.

"Tomorrow I'll ride in and have a look around. You'd better keep the other men close by."

Dawn found him well along on the trail to Yellow Jacket. It was a long ride, and he skirted the trail most of the time, having no trust in well-traveled ways at such a time. The air was warm and bright, and he noticed a few head of Pivotrock steers that had been overlooked in the rounding up of cattle along the rim.

He rode ready for trouble, his Winchester across his saddle bows, his senses alert. Keeping the roan well back under the trees, he had the benefit of the evergreen needles that formed a thick carpet and muffled the sound of his horse's hoofs.

Yet, as he rode, he considered the problem of the land grant. If Jenny were to retain her land and be free of trouble, he must look into the background of the grant and see which had the prior and best claim, Fernandez or Sonoma.

Next, he must find out, if possible, where Bill Curtin had obtained that five thousand dollars. Some might think that the fact he had it was enough and that now his wife had it, but it was not enough if Bill had sold any rights to water or land on the ranch or if he had obtained the money in some way that would reflect upon Jenny or her son.

When those things were done, he could ride on about his business, for by that time he would have worked out the problem of Galusha Reed.

In the few days he had been on the Pivotrock, he had come to love the place, and, while he had avoided Jenny, he had not avoided young Billy. The youngster had adopted him and had stayed with him hour after hour.

To keep him occupied, Matt had begun teaching him how to plait rawhide, and so, as he mended reatas and repaired bridles, the youngster had sat beside him, working his fingers clumsily through the intricacies of the plaiting.

It was with unease that he recalled his few minutes alone with Jenny. He shifted his seat in the saddle and scowled. It would not do for him to think of her as anything but Curtin's widow. The widow, he reflected bitterly, of the man he had killed.

What would he say when she learned of that? He avoided the thought, yet it remained in the back of his mind, and he shook his head, wanting to forget it. Sooner or later, she would know. If he did not finally tell her himself, then he was sure that Reed would let her know.

Avoiding the route by way of Hardscrabble, Matt Sabre turned due south, crossing the eastern end of the mesa and following an old trail across Whiterock and Polles Mesa, crossing the East Verde at Rock Creek. Then he cut through Boardinghouse Cañon to Bullspring, crossing the main stream of the Verde near Tangle Peak. It was a longer way around by a few miles, but Sabre rode with care, watching the country as he traveled. It was very late when he walked his roan into the parched street of Yellow Jacket.

He had a hunch and he meant to follow it through. During his nights in the bunkhouse he had talked much with Judson, and from him heard of Pepito Fernandez, a grandson of the man who had sold the land to Old Man Curtin.

Swinging down from his horse at the livery stable, he led him inside.

Simpson walked over to meet him, his eyes searching Sabre's face. "Man, you've a nerve with you. Reed's wild. He came back to town blazing mad, and Trumbull's telling everybody what you can expect."

Matt smiled at the man. "I expected that. Where do you stand?"

"Well," Simpson said grimly, "I've no liking for Trumbull. He carries himself mighty big around town, and he's not been friendly to me and mine. I reckon, mister, I've rare been so pleased as when you made a fool of him in yonder. It was better than the killing of him, although he's that coming, sure enough."

"Then take care of my horse, will you? And a slipknot to tie him with."

"Sure, and he'll get corn, too. I reckon any horse you ride would need corn."

Matt Sabre walked out on the street. He was wearing dark jeans and a gray wool shirt. His black hat was pulled low, and he merged well with the shadows. He'd see Pepito first, and then look around a bit. He wanted Camp Gordon.

Thinking of that, he turned back into the stable. "Saddle Gordon's horse, too. He'll be going back with me."

"Him?" Simpson stared. "Man, he's dead drunk and has been for days!"

"Saddle his horse. He'll be with me when I'm back, and, if you know another one or two good hands who would use a gun if need be, let them know I'm hiring and there's money to pay them. Fighting wages if they want."

In the back office of the Yellow Jacket, three men sat around Galusha Reed's desk. There was Reed himself, Sid Trumbull, and Prince McCarran.

"Do you think Tony can take him?" Reed asked. "You've seen the man draw, Prince."

"He'll take him. But it will be close . . . too close. I think what we'd better do is have Sid posted somewhere close by."

"Leave me out of it." Sid looked up from under his thick eyebrows. "I want no more of the man. Let Tony have him."

"You won't be in sight," McCarran said dryly, "or in danger. You'll be upstairs over the hotel, with a Winchester."

Trumbull looked up and touched his thick lips with his tongue. Killing was not new to him, yet the way this man accepted it always appalled him a little.

"All right," he agreed. "Like I say, I've no love for him."

"We'll have him so you'll get a flanking shot. Make it count and make it the first time. But wait until the shooting starts."

The door opened softly, and Sikes stepped in. He was a lithe, dark-skinned man who moved like an animal. He had graceful hands, restless hands. He wore a white buckskin vest worked with red quills and beads. "Boss, he's in town. Sabre's here." He had heard them.

Reed let his chair legs down, leaning forward. "Here? In town?"

"That's right. I just saw him outside the Yellow Jacket." Sikes started to build a cigarette. "He's got nerve. Plenty of it."

The door sounded with a light tap, and at a word Keys entered. He was a slight man with gray hair and a quiet scholar's face.

"I remember him now, Prince," he said. "Matt

Sabre. I'd been trying to place the name. He was marshal of Mobeetie for a while. He's killed eight or nine men."

"That's right!" Trumbull looked up sharply. "Mobeetie! Why didn't I remember that? They say Wes Hardin rode out of town once when Sabre sent him word he wasn't wanted."

Sikes turned his eyes on McCarran. "You want him now?"

McCarran hesitated, studying the polished toe of his boot. Sabre's handling of Trumbull had made friends in town, as had his championing of the cause of Jenny Curtin. Whatever happened must be seemingly aboveboard and in the clear, and he wanted to be where he could be seen at the time, and Reed, also.

"No, not now. We'll wait." He smiled. "One thing about a man of his courage and background, if you send for him, he'll always come to you."

"But how will he come?" Keys asked softly. "That's the question."

McCarran looked around irritably. He had forgotten Keys was in the room and had said far more than he had intended. "Thanks, Keys. That will be all. And remember . . . nothing will be said about anything you've heard here."

"Certainly not." Keys smiled and walked to the door and out of the room.

Reed stared after him. "I don't like that fellow, Prince. I wouldn't trust him."

"Him? He's interested in nothing but that piano and enough liquor to keep himself mildly embalmed. Don't worry about him."

IV

Matt Sabre turned away from the Yellow Jacket after a brief survey of the saloon. Obviously something was doing elsewhere for none of the men was present in the big room. He hesitated, considering the significance of that, and then turned down a dark alleyway and walked briskly along until he came to an old rail fence.

Following this past rustling cottonwoods and down a rutted road, he turned past a barn and cut across another road toward an adobe where the windows glowed with a faint light.

The door opened to his knock, and a dark, Indian-like face showed briefly. In rapid Spanish he asked for Pepito. After a moment's hesitation, the door widened, and he was invited inside.

The room was large, and at one side a small fire burned in the blackened fireplace. An oilcloth-covered table with a coal-oil light stood in the middle of the room, and on a bed at one side a man snored peacefully.

A couple of dark-eyed children ceased their

playing to look up at him. The woman called out, and a blanket pushed aside, and a slender, dark-faced youth entered the room, pulling his belt tight.

"Pepito Fernandez? I am Matt Sabre."

"I have heard of you, *señor*."

Briefly he explained why he had come, and Pepito listened, then shook his head. "I do not know, *señor*. The grant was long ago, and we are no longer rich. My father"—he shrugged—"he liked the spending of money when he was young." He hesitated, considering that. Then he said carelessly: "I, too, like the spending of money. What else is it for? But no, *señor*, I do not think there are papers. My father, he told me much of the grant, and I am sure the Sonomas had no strong claim."

"If you remember anything, will you let us know?" Sabre asked. Then a thought occurred to him. "You're a *vaquero*? Do you want a job?"

"A job?" Pepito studied him thoughtfully. "At the *Señora* Curtin's ranch?"

"Yes. As you know, there may be much trouble. I am working there, and tonight I shall take one other man back with me. If you would like the job, it is yours."

Pepito shrugged. "Why not? *Señor* Curtin, the old one, he gave me my first horse. He gave me a rifle, too. He was a good one, and the son, also."

53

"Better meet me outside of town where the trail goes between the buttes. You know the place?"

"*Sí, señor*. I will be there."

Keys was idly playing the piano when Matt Sabre opened the door and stepped into the room. His quick eyes placed Keys, Hobbs at the bar, Camp Gordon fast asleep with his head on a table, and a half dozen other men. Yet, as he walked to the bar, a rear door opened, and Tony Sikes stepped into the room.

Sabre had never before seen the man, yet he knew him from Judson's apt and careful description. Sikes was not as tall as Sabre, yet more slender. He had the wiry, stringy build that is made for speed, and quick, smooth-flowing fingers. His muscles were relaxed and easy, but knowing such men Matt recognized danger when he saw it. Sikes had seen him at once, and he moved to the bar nearby.

All eyes were on the two of them, for the story of Matt's whipping of Trumbull and his defiance of Reed had swept the country. Yet Sikes merely smiled and Matt glanced at him. "Have a drink?"

Tony Sikes nodded. "I don't mind if I do." Then he added, his voice low and his dark, yellowish eyes on Matt's with a faintly sardonic, faintly amused look: "I never mind drinking with a man I'm going to kill."

Sabre shrugged. "Neither do I." He found himself liking Sikes's direct approach. "Although perhaps I have the advantage. I choose my own time to drink and to kill. You wait for orders."

Tony Sikes felt in his vest pocket for cigarette papers and began to roll a smoke. "You will wait for me, *compadre*. I know you're the type."

They drank, and, as they drank, the door opened, and Galusha Reed stepped out. His face darkened angrily when he saw the two standing at the bar together, but he was passing without speaking when a thought struck him. He stopped and turned.

"I wonder," he said loudly enough for all in the room to hear, "what Jenny Curtin will say when she finds out her new hand is the man who killed her husband?"

Every head came up, and Sabre's face whitened. Whereas the faces had been friendly or non-committal, now they were sharp-eyed and attentive. Moreover, he knew that Jenny was well liked, as Curtin had been. Now they would be his enemies,

"I wonder just why you came here, Sabre? After killing the girl's husband, why would you come to her ranch? Was it to profit from your murder? To steal what little she has left? Or is it for the girl herself?"

Matt struggled to keep his temper. After a minute, he said casually: "Reed, it was you ordered her off her ranch. I'm here for one reason, and one alone. To see that she keeps her ranch and that no yellow-bellied, thievin' lot of coyotes ride over and take it away from her."

Reed stood flat-footed, facing Sabre. He was furious, and Matt could feel the force of his rage. It was almost a physical thing pushing against him. Close beside him was Sikes. If Reed chose to go for a gun, Sikes could grab Matt's left arm and jerk him off balance. Yet Matt was ready even for that, and again that black force was rising within him, that driving urge toward violence.

He spoke again, and his voice was soft and almost purring. "Make up your mind, Reed. If you want to die, you can right here. You make another remark to me and I'll drive every word of it back down that fat throat of yours. Reach, and I'll kill you. If Sikes wants in on this, he's welcome."

Tony Sikes spoke softly, too. "I'm out of it, Sabre. I only fight my own battles. When I come after you, I'll be alone."

Galusha Reed hesitated. For an instant, counting on Sikes, he had been tempted. Now he hesitated, then turned abruptly and left the room.

Ignoring Sikes, Sabre downed his drink and crossed to Camp Gordon. He shook him. "Come on, Camp. I'm putting you to bed."

56

Gordon did not move. Sabre stooped and slipped an arm around the big Englishman's shoulders and, hoisting him to his feet, started for the door. At the door, he turned. "I'll be seeing you, Sikes."

Tony lifted his glass, his hat pushed back. "Sure," he said. "And I'll be alone."

It was not until after he had said it that he remembered Sid Trumbull and the plans made in the back room. His face darkened a little, and his liquor suddenly tasted bad. He put his glass down carefully on the bar and turned, walking through the back door.

Prince McCarran was alone, idly riffling the cards and smoking. "I won't do it, Prince," Sikes said. "You've got to leave that killing to me and me alone."

Matt Sabre, with Camp Gordon lashed to the saddle of a led horse, met Pepito in the darkness of the space between the buttes. Pepito spoke softly, and Sabre called back to him. As the Mexican rode out, he glanced once at Gordon, and then the three rode on together. It was late the following morning when they reached the Pivotrock.

Camp Gordon was sober and swearing. "Shanghaied!" His voice exploded with violence. "You've a nerve, Sabre. Turn me loose so I can start back. I'm having no part of this."

Gordon was tied to his horse so he would not fall off, but Matt only grinned. "Sure, I'll turn you loose. But you said you ought to get out of town a while, and this was the best way. I've brought you here," he said gravely, but his eyes were twinkling, "for your own good. It's time you had some fresh, mountain air, some cold milk, some . . ."

"Milk?" Gordon exploded. "Milk, you say? I'll not touch the stuff! Turn me loose and give me a gun and I'll have your hide!"

"And leave this ranch for Reed to take? Reed and McCarran?"

Gordon stared at him from bloodshot eyes, eyes that were suddenly attentive. "Did you say McCarran? What's he got to do with this?"

"I wish I knew. But I've a hunch he's in up to his ears. I think he has strings on Reed."

Gordon considered that. "He may have." He watched Sabre undoing the knots. "It's a point I hadn't considered. But why?"

"You've known him longer than I have. Somebody had two men follow Curtin out of the country to kill him, and I don't believe Reed did it. Does that make sense?"

"No." Gordon swung stiffly to the ground. He swayed a bit, clinging to the stirrup leather. He glanced sheepishly at Matt. "I guess I'm a mess." A surprised look crossed his face. "Say, I'm hungry! I haven't been hungry in weeks."

• • •

With four hands besides himself, work went on swiftly. Yet Matt Sabre's mind would not rest. The five thousand dollars was a problem, and also there was the grant. Night after night, he led Pepito to talk of the memories of his father and grandfather, and little by little he began to know the men. An idea was shaping in his mind, but as yet there was little on which to build.

In all this time, there was no sign of Reed. On two occasions, riders had been seen, apparently scouting. Cattle had been swept from the rim edge and pushed back, accounting for all or nearly all the strays he had seen on his ride to Yellow Jacket.

Matt was restless, sure that when trouble came, it would come with a rush. It was like Reed to do things that way. By now he was certainly aware that Camp Gordon and Pepito Fernandez had been added to the roster of hands at Pivotrock.

"Spotted a few head over near Baker Butte," Camp said one morning. "How'd it be if I drifted that way and looked them over?"

"We'll go together," Matt replied. "I've been wanting to look around there, and there's been no chance."

The morning was bright, and they rode swiftly, putting miles behind them, alert to all the sights and sounds of the high country above the rim. Careful as they were, they were no more than one hundred yards from the riders when they saw them. There were five men, and in the lead rode Sid Trumbull and a white-mustached stranger.

There was no possibility of escaping unnoticed. They pushed on toward the advancing riders, who drew up and waited.

Sid Trumbull's face was sharp with triumph when he saw Sabre. "Here's your man, Marshal!" he said with satisfaction. "The one with the black hat is Sabre."

"What's this all about?" Matt asked quietly. He had already noticed the badge the man wore. But he noticed something else. The man looked to be a competent, upstanding officer.

"You're wanted in El Paso. I'm Rafe Collins, deputy United States marshal. We're making an inquiry into the killing of Bill Curtin."

Camp's lips tightened, and he looked sharply at Sabre. When Reed had brought out this fact in the saloon, Gordon had been dead drunk.

"That was a fair shooting, Marshal. Curtin picked the fight and drew on me."

"You expect us to believe that?" Trumbull was contemptuous. "Why, he hadn't the courage of a mouse! He backed down from Sikes only a few days before. He wouldn't draw on any man with two hands!"

"He drew on me." Matt Sabre realized he was fighting two battles here—one to keep from being arrested, the other to keep Gordon's respect and assistance. "My idea is that he only backed out of a fight with Sikes because he had a job to do and knew Sikes would kill him."

"That's a likely yarn!" Trumbull nodded. "There's your man. It's your job, Marshal."

Collins was obviously irritated. That he entertained no great liking for Trumbull was obvious. Yet he had his duty to do. Before he could speak, Sabre spoke again.

"Marshal, I've reason to believe that some influence has been brought to bear to discredit me and to get me out of the country for a while. Can't I give you my word that I'll report to El Paso when things are straightened out? My word is good, and there are many in El Paso who know that."

"Sorry." Collins was regretful. "I've my duty and my orders."

"I understand that," Sabre replied. "I also have my duty. It is to see that Jenny Curtin is protected from those who are trying to force her off her range. I intend to do exactly that."

"Your duty?" Collins eyed him coldly but curiously. "After killing her husband?"

"That's reason enough, sir," Sabre replied flatly. "The fight was not my choice. Curtin pushed it, and he was excited, worried, and overwrought. Yet he asked me on his deathbed to deliver a package to his wife and to see that

61

she was protected. That duty, sir"—his eyes met those of Collins—"comes first."

"I'd like to respect that," Collins admitted. "You seem like a gentleman, sir, and it's a quality that's too rare. Unfortunately, I have my orders. However, it should not take long to straighten this out if it was a fair shooting."

"All these rats need," Sabre replied, "is a few days." He knew there was no use arguing. His horse was fast, and dense pines bordered the road. He needed a minute, and that badly.

As if divining his thought, Camp Gordon suddenly pushed his gray between Matt and the marshal, and almost at once Matt lashed out with his toe and booted Trumbull's horse in the ribs. The bronco went to bucking furiously. Whipping his horse around, Matt slapped the spurs to his ribs, and in two startled jumps he was off and deep into the pines, running like a startled deer.

Behind him a shot rang out, and then another. Both cut the brush over his head, but the horse was running now, and he was mounted well. He had started into the trees at right angles but swung his horse immediately and headed back toward the Pivotrock. Corduroy Wash opened off to his left, and he turned the black and pushed rapidly into the mouth of the wash.

Following it for almost a mile, he came out and paused briefly in the clump of trees that crowned a small ridge. He stared back.

A string of riders stretched out on his back trail, but they were scattered out, hunting for tracks. A lone horseman sat not far from them, obviously watching. Matt grinned. That would be Gordon, and he was all right.

Turning his horse, Matt followed a shelf of rock until it ran out, rode off it into thick sand, and then into the pines with their soft bed of needles that left almost no tracks.

Cinch Hook Butte was off to his left, and nearer, on his right, Twenty-Nine-Mile Butte. Keeping his horse headed between them, but bearing steadily northwest, he headed for the broken country around Horsetank Wash. Descending into the cañon, he rode northwest, then circled back south, and entered the even deeper Calfpen Cañon.

Here, in a nest of boulders, he staked out his horse on a patch of grass. Rifle across his knees, he rested. After an hour, he worked his way to the ledge at the top of the cañon, but nowhere could he see any sign of pursuit. Nor could he hear the sound of hoofs.

There was water in the bottom of Calfpen, not far from where he had left his horse. Food was something else again. He shucked a handful of chia seeds and ate a handful of them, along with the nuts of a piñon.

Obviously the attempted arrest had been brought about by either the influence of Galusha

Reed or Prince McCarran. In either case, he was now a fugitive. If they went on to the ranch, Rafe Collins would have a chance to talk to Jenny Curtin. Matt felt sick when he thought of the marshal telling her that it was he who had killed her husband. That she must find out sooner or later, he knew, but he wanted to tell her himself, in his own good time.

V

When dusk had fallen, he mounted the black and worked his way down Calfpen toward Fossil Springs. As he rode, he was considering his best course. Whether taken by Collins or not, he was not now at the ranch and they might choose this time to strike. With some reason, they might believe he had left the country. Indeed, there was every chance that Reed actually believed he had come there with some plan of his own to get the Curtin ranch.

Finally, he bedded down for the night in a draw above Fossil Springs and slept soundly until daylight brought a sun that crept over the rocks and shone upon his eyes. He was up, made a light breakfast of coffee and jerked beef, and then saddled up.

Wherever he went now, he could expect hostility. Doubt or downright suspicion would have developed as a result of Reed's accusation in Yellow Jacket, and the country would know the U.S. marshal was looking for him.

Debating his best course, Matt Sabre headed west through the mountains. By nightfall the following day, he was camped in the ominous shadow of Turret Butte where only a few years before Major Randall had ascended the peak in darkness to surprise a camp of Apaches.

Awakening at the break of dawn, Matt scouted the vicinity of Yellow Jacket with care.

There was some movement in town—more than usual at that hour. He observed a long line of saddled horses at the hitch rails. He puzzled over this, studying it with narrowed eyes from the crest of a ridge through his glasses. Marshal Collins could not yet have returned, hence this must be some other movement. That it was organized was obvious.

He was still watching when a man wearing a faded red shirt left the back door of a building near the saloon, went to a horse carefully hidden in the rear, and mounted. At this distance, there was no way of seeing who he was. The man rode strangely. Studying him through the glasses—a relic of Sabre's military years—Matt suddenly realized why the rider seemed strange. He was riding Eastern fashion!

This was no Westerner, slouched and lazy in the saddle, nor yet sitting upright as a cavalryman might. This man rode forward on his horse, a poor practice for the hard miles of desert or mountain riding. Yet it was his surreptitious manner rather than his riding style that intrigued Matt. It required but a few minutes for Matt to see that the route the rider was taking away from town would bring him by near the base of the promontory where he watched.

Reluctant as he was to give over watching the saddled horses, Sabre was sure this strange rider held some clue to his problems. Sliding back on his belly well into the brush, Matt got to his feet and descended the steep trail and took up his place among the boulders beside the trail.

It was very hot there out of the breeze, yet he had waited only a minute until he heard the sound of the approaching horse. He cleared his gun from its holster and moved to the very edge of the road. Then the rider appeared. It was Keys.

Matt's gun stopped him. "Where you riding, Keys?" Matt asked quietly. "What's this all about?"

"I'm riding to intercept the marshal," Keys said sincerely. "McCarran and Reed plan to send out a posse of their own men to hunt you, then, under cover of capturing you, they intend to take the Pivotrock and hold it."

Sabre nodded. That would be it, of course, and he should have guessed it before. "What about the marshal? They'll run into him on the trail."

"No, they're going to swing south of his trail. They know how he's riding because Reed is guiding him."

"What's your stake in this? Why ride all the way out there to tell the marshal?"

"It's because of Jenny Curtin," he said frankly. "She's a fine girl, and Bill was a good boy. Both of them treated me fine, as their father did before them. It's little enough to do, and I know too much about the plotting of that devil McCarran."

"Then it is McCarran. Where does Reed stand in this?"

"He's stupid," Keys said contemptuously. "McCarran is using him, and he hasn't the wit to see it. He believes they are partners, but Prince will get rid of him like he does anyone who gets in his way. He'll be rid of Trumbull, too."

"And Sikes?"

"Perhaps. Sikes is a good tool, to a point."

Matt Sabre shoved his hat back on his head. "Keys," he said suddenly, "I want you to have a little faith in me. Believe me, I'm doing what I can to help Jenny Curtin. I did kill her husband, but he was a total stranger who was edgy and started a fight.

"I'd no way of knowing who or what he was, and the gun of a stranger kills as easy as the gun of a known man. But he trusted me. He asked me to come here, to bring his wife five thousand, and to help her."

"Five thousand?" Keys stared. "Where did he get that amount of money?"

"I'd like to know," Sabre admitted. Another idea occurred to him. "Keys, you know more about what's going on in this town than anyone else. What do you know about the Sonoma Grant?"

Keys hesitated, then said slowly: "Sabre, I know very little about that. I think the only one who has the true facts is Prince McCarran. I think he gathered all the available papers on both grants and is sure that no matter what his claim, the grant cannot be substantiated. Nobody knows but McCarran."

"Then I'll go to McCarran," Sabre replied harshly. "I'm going to straighten this out if it's the last thing I do."

"You go to McCarran and it will be the last thing you do. The man's deadly. He's smooth-talking and treacherous. And then there's Sikes."

"Yes," Sabre admitted. "There's Sikes." He studied the situation, then looked up. "Don't you bother the marshal. Leave him to me. Every man he's got with him is an enemy to Jenny Curtin, and they would never let you talk. You circle them and ride on to Pivotrock. You tell Camp Gordon what's happening. Tell him of this outfit that's saddled up. I'll do my job here, and then I'll start back."

Long after Keys had departed, Sabre watched.

Evidently the posse was awaiting some word from Reed. Would McCarran ride with them? He was too careful. He would wait in Yellow Jacket. He would be, as always, an innocent bystander. . . .

Keys, riding up the trail some miles distant, drew up suddenly. He had forgotten to tell Sabre of Prince McCarran's plan to have Sid Trumbull cut him down when he tangled with Sikes. For a long moment, Keys sat his horse, staring worriedly and scowling. To go back now would lose time; moreover, there was small chance that Sabre would be there. Matt Sabre would have to take his own chances.

Regretfully Keys pushed on into the rough country ahead. . . .

Tony Sikes found McCarran seated in the back room at the saloon. McCarran glanced up quickly as he came in, and then nodded.

"Glad to see you, Sikes. I want you close by. I think we'll have visitors today or tomorrow."

"Visitors?" Sikes searched McCarran's face.

"A visitor, I should say. I think we'll see Matt Sabre."

Tony Sikes considered that, turning it over in his mind. Yes, Prince was right. Sabre would not surrender. It would be like him to head for town, hunting Reed. Aside from three or four men, nobody knew of McCarran's connection with the Pivotrock affair. Reed and Trumbull were fronting for him.

Trumbull, Reed, Sikes, and Keys. Keys was a shrewd man. He might be a drunk and a piano player, but he had a head on his shoulders.

Sikes's mind leaped suddenly. Keys was not around. This was the first time in weeks that he had not encountered Keys in the bar.

Keys was gone.

Where would he go—to warn Jenny Curtin of the posse? So what? He had nothing against Jenny Curtin. He was a man who fought for hire. Maybe he was on the wrong side in this. Even as he thought of that, he remembered Matt Sabre. The man was sharp as a steel blade—trim, fast. Now that it had been recalled to his mind, he remembered all that he had heard of him as marshal of Mobeetie.

There was in Tony Sikes a drive that forbade him to admit any man was his fighting superior. Sabre's draw against Trumbull was still the talk of the town—talk that irked Sikes, for folks were beginning to compare the two of them. Many thought Sabre might be faster. That rankled.

He would meet Sabre first and then drift.

"Don't you think he'll get here?" McCarran asked, looking up at Tony.

Sikes nodded. "He'll get here, all right. He thinks too fast for Trumbull or Reed. Even for that marshal."

Sikes would have Sabre to himself. Sid Trumbull was out of town. Tony Sikes wanted to do his own killing.

Matt Sabre watched the saddled horses. He had that quality of patience so long associated with the Indian. He knew how to wait and how to relax. He waited now, letting all his muscles rest. With all his old alertness for danger—his sixth sense that warned him of climaxes—he knew this situation had reached the explosion point.

The marshal would be returning. Reed and Trumbull would be sure that he did not encounter the posse. And that body of riders, most of whom were henchmen or cronies of Galusha Reed, would sweep down on the Pivotrock and capture it, killing all who were there under the pretense of searching for Matt Sabre.

Keys would warn them, and in time. Once they knew of the danger, Camp Gordon and the others would be wise enough to take the necessary precautions. The marshal was one tentacle, but there in Yellow Jacket was the heart of the trouble.

If Prince McCarran and Tony Sikes were removed, the tentacles would shrivel and die. Despite the danger out at Pivotrock, high behind the Mogollon Rim, the decisive blow must be struck right here in Yellow Jacket.

He rolled over on his stomach and lifted the

glasses. Men were coming from the Yellow Jacket Saloon and mounting up. Lying at his ease, he watched them go. There were at least thirty, possibly more. When they had gone, he got to his feet and brushed off his clothes. Then he walked slowly down to his horse and mounted.

He rode quietly, one hand lying on his thigh, his eyes alert, his brain relaxed and ready for impressions.

Marshal Rafe Collins was a just man. He was a frontiersman, a man who knew the West and the men it bred. He was no fool—shrewd and careful, rigid in his enforcement of the law, yet wise in the ways of men. Moreover, he was Southern in the oldest of Southern traditions, and, being so, he understood what Matt Sabre meant when he said it was because he had killed her husband that he must protect Jenny Curtin.

Matt Sabre left his horse at the livery stable. Simpson looked up sharply when he saw him.

"You better watch yourself," he warned. "The whole country's after you, an' they are huntin' blood!"

"I know. What about Sikes? Is he in town?"

"Sure! He never leaves McCarran." Simpson searched his face. "Sikes is no man to tangle with, Sabre. He's chain lightnin'."

"I know." Sabre watched his horse led into a shadowed stall. Then he turned to Simpson. "You've been friendly, Simpson. I like that.

After today, there's going to be a new order of things around here, but today I could use some help. What do you know about the Pivotrock deal?"

The man hesitated, chewing slowly. Finally he spat and looked up. "There was nobody to tell until now," he said, "but two things I know. That grant was Curtin's, all right, an' he wasn't killed by accident. He was murdered."

"Murdered?"

"Yeah." Simpson's expression was wry. "Like you, he liked fancy drinkin' liquor when he could get it. McCarran was right friendly. He asked Curtin to have a drink with him that day, an' Curtin did.

"On'y a few minutes after that, he came in here an' got a team to drive back, leavin' his horse in here because it had gone lame. I watched him climb into that rig, an' he missed the step an' almost fell on his face. Then he finally managed to climb in."

"Drunk?" Sabre's eyes were alert and interested.

"Him?" Simpson snorted. "That old coot could stow away more liquor than a turkey could corn. He had only one drink, yet he could hardly walk."

"Doped, then?" Sabre nodded. That sounded like McCarran. "And then what?"

"When the team was brought back after they ran away with him, an' after Curtin was found dead, I found a bullet graze on the hip of one of those broncos."

So that was how it had been. A doped man, a skittish team of horses, and a bullet to burn the horse just enough to start it running. Prince McCarran was a thorough man.

"You said you knew that Curtin really owned that grant. How?"

Simpson shrugged. "Because he had that other claim investigated. He must have heard rumors of trouble. There'd been talk of it that I heard, an' here a man hears everythin'!

"Anyway, he had all the papers with him when he started back to the ranch that day. He showed 'em to me earlier. All the proof."

"And he was murdered that day? Who found the body?"

"Sid Trumbull. He was ridin' that way, sort of accidental like."

The proof Jenny needed was in the hands of Prince McCarran. By all means, he must call on Prince.

VI

Matt Sabre walked to the door and stood there, waiting a moment in the shadow before emerging into the sunlight.

The street was dusty and curiously empty.

The rough-fronted gray buildings of unpainted lumber or sand-colored adobe faced him blankly from across and up the street. The hitch rail was deserted; the water trough overflowed a little, making a darkening stain under one end.

Somewhere up the street, but behind the buildings, a hen began proclaiming her egg to the hemispheres. A single white cloud hung lazily in the blue sky. Matt stepped out. Hitching his gun belts a little, he looked up the street.

Sikes would be in the Yellow Jacket. To see McCarran, he must see Sikes first. That was the way he wanted it. One thing at a time.

He was curiously quiet. He thought of other times when he had faced such situations— of Mobeetie, of that first day out on the plains hunting buffalo, of the first time he had killed a man, of a charge the Riffs had made on a small desert patrol out of Taudeni long ago.

A faint breeze stirred an old sack that lay near the boardwalk, and farther up the street, near the water trough, a long gray rat slipped out from under a store and headed toward the drip of water from the trough. Matt Sabre started to walk, moving up the street.

It was not far, as distance goes, but there is no walk as long as the gunman's walk, no pause as long as the pause before gunfire. On this day, Sikes would know, instantly, what his presence here presaged. McCarran would know, too.

Prince McCarran was not a gambler. He would scarcely trust all to Tony Sikes no matter how confident he might be. It always paid to have something to back up a facing card. Trust Prince to keep his hole card well covered. But on this occasion, he would not be bluffing. He would have a hole card, but where? How? What? And when?

The last was not hard. When—the moment of the gun battle.

He had walked no more than thirty yards when a door creaked and a man stepped into the street. He did not look down toward Sabre but walked briskly to the center of the street, then faced about sharply like a man on a parade ground.

Tony Sikes.

He wore this day a faded blue shirt that stretched tightly over his broad, bony shoulders and fell slackly in front where his chest was hollow and his stomach flat. It was too far yet to see his eyes, but Matt Sabre knew what they looked like.

The thin, angular face, the mustache, the high cheek bones, and the long, restless fingers. The man's hips were narrow, and there was little enough to his body. Tony Sikes lifted his eyes and stared down the street. His lips were dry, but he felt ready. There was a curious lightness within him, but he liked it so, and he liked the set-up.

76

At that moment, he felt almost an affection for Sabre.

The man knew so well the rules of the game. He was coming as he should come, and there was something about him—an edged quality, a poised and alert strength.

No sound penetrated the clear globe of stillness. The warm air hung still, with even the wind poised, arrested by the drama in the street. Matt Sabre felt a slow trickle of sweat start from under his hatband. He walked carefully, putting each foot down with care and distinction of purpose. It was Tony Sikes who stopped first, some sixty yards away.

"Well, Matt, here it is. We both knew it was coming."

"Sure." Matt paused, too, feet apart, hands swinging widely. "You tied up with the wrong outfit, Sikes."

"We'd have met, anyway." Sikes looked along the street at the tall man standing there, looked and saw his bronzed face, hard and ready. It was not in Sikes to feel fear of a man with guns. Yet this was how he would die. It was in the cards. He smiled suddenly. Yes, he would die by the gun—but not now.

His hands stirred, and, as if their movement was a signal to his muscles, they flashed in a draw. Before him, the dark, tall figure flashed suddenly. It was no more than that, a blur of movement and a lifted gun, a movement suddenly stilled, and the black sullen muzzle of a six-gun that steadied on him even as he cleared his gun from his open top holster.

He had been beaten—beaten to the draw.

The shock of it triggered Sikes's gun, and he knew even as the gun bucked in his hand that he had missed, and then suddenly Matt Sabre was running! Running toward him, gun lifted, but not firing!

In a panic, Sikes saw the distance closing and he fired as fast as he could pull the trigger, three times in a thundering cascade of sound. And even as the hammer fell for the fourth shot, he heard another gun bellow.

But where? There had been no stab of flame from Sabre's gun. Sabre was running, a rapidly moving target, and Sikes had fired too fast, upset by the sudden rush, by the panic of realizing he had been beaten to the draw.

He lifted his right-hand gun, dropped the muzzle in a careful arc, and saw Sabre's skull over the barrel. Then Sabre skidded to a halt, and his gun hammered bullets.

Flame leaped from the muzzle, stabbing at Sikes, burning him along the side, making his body twitch and the bullet go wild. He switched guns, and then something slugged him in the wind, and the next he knew he was on the ground.

Matt Sabre had heard that strange shot, but

that was another thing. He could not wait now; he could not turn his attention. He saw Sikes go down, but only to his knees, and the gunman had five bullets and the range now was only fifteen yards.

Sikes's gun swung up, and Matt fired again. Sikes lunged to his feet, and then his features writhed with agony and breathlessness, and he went down, hard to the ground, twisting in the dust.

Then another bullet bellowed, and a shot kicked up dust at his feet. Matt swung his gun and blasted at an open window, then started for the saloon door. He stopped, hearing a loud cry behind him.

"Matt Sabre?"

It was Sikes, his eyes flared widely. Sabre hesitated, glanced swiftly around, then dropped to his knees in the silent street.

"What is it, Tony? Anything I can do for you?"

"Behind . . . behind . . . the desk . . . you . . . you . . ." His faltering voice faded, then strength seemed to flood back, and he looked up. "Good man! Too . . . too fast!"

And then he was dead, gone just like that, and Matt Sabre was striding into the Yellow Jacket.

The upstairs room was empty; the stairs were empty; there was no one in sight. Only Hobbs stood behind the bar when he came down. Hobbs, his face set and pale.

Sabre looked at him, eyes steady and cold. "Who came down those stairs?"

Hobbs licked his lips. He choked, then whispered hoarsely: "Nobody . . . but there's . . . there's a back stairs."

Sabre wheeled and walked back in quick strides, thumbing shells into his gun. The office door was open, and Prince McCarran looked up as he framed himself in the door.

He was writing, and the desk was rumpled with papers, the desk of a busy man. Nearby was a bottle and a full glass.

McCarran lay down his pen. "So? You beat him? I thought you might."

"Did you?" Sabre's gaze was cold. If this man had been running, as he must have run, he gave no evidence of it now. "You should hire them faster, Prince."

"Well"—McCarran shrugged—"he was fast enough until now. But this wasn't my job, anyway. He was workin' for Reed."

Sabre took a step inside the door, away from the wall, keeping his hands free. His eyes were on those of Prince McCarran, and Prince watched him, alert, interested.

"That won't ride with me," Matt said. "Reed's a stooge, a perfect stooge. He'll be lucky if he comes back alive from this trip. A lot of that posse you sent out won't come back, either."

McCarran's eyelids tightened at the mention of

80

the posse. "Forget it." He waved his hand. "Sit down and have a drink. After all, we're not fools, Sabre. We're grown men, and we can talk. I never liked killing, anyway."

"Unless you do it or have it done." Sabre's hands remained where they were. "What's the matter, Prince? Yellow? Afraid to do your own killing?"

McCarran's face was still, and his eyes were wide now. "You shouldn't have said that. You shouldn't have called me yellow."

"Then get on your feet. I hate to shoot a sitting man."

"Have a drink and let's talk."

"Sure." Sabre was elaborately casual. "You have one, too." He reached his hand for the glass that had already been poured, but McCarran's eyes were steady. Sabre switched his hand and grasped the other glass, and then, like a striking snake, Prince McCarran grasped his right hand and jerked him forward, off balance.

At the same time, McCarran's left flashed back to the holster high on his left side, butt forward, and the gun jerked up and free. Matt Sabre, instead of trying to jerk his right hand free, let his weight go forward, following and hurling himself against McCarran. The chair went over with a crash, and Prince tried to straighten, but Matt was riding him back. He crashed into the wall, and Sabre broke free.

Prince swung his gun up, and Sabre's left palm slapped down, knocking the gun aside and gripping the hand across the thumb. His right hand came up under the gun barrel, twisting it back over and out of McCarran's hands. Then he shoved him back and dropped the gun, slapping him across the mouth with his open palm.

It was a free swing, and it cracked like a pistol shot. McCarran's face went white from the blow, and he rushed, swinging, but Sabre brought up his knee in the charging man's groin. Then he smashed him in the face with his elbow, pushing him over and back. McCarran dived past him, blood streaming from his crushed nose, and grabbed wildly at the papers. His hand came up with a bulldog .41.

Matt saw the hand shoot for the papers, and, even as the .41 appeared, his own gun was lifting. He fired first, three times, at a range of four feet.

Prince McCarran stiffened, lifted to his tiptoes, then plunged over on his face, and lay still among the litter of papers and broken glass.

Sabre swayed drunkenly. He recalled what Sikes had said about the desk. He caught the edge and jerked it aside, swinging the desk away from the wall. Behind it was a small panel with a knob. It was locked, but a bullet smashed the lock. He jerked it open. A thick wad of bills, a small sack of gold coins, a sheaf of papers.

A glance sufficed. These were the papers

Simpson had mentioned. The thick parchment of the original grant, the information on the conflicting Sonoma grant, and then . . . He glanced swiftly through them, then, at a pound of horses' hoofs, he stuffed them inside his shirt. He stopped, stared. His shirt was soaked with blood.

Fumbling, he got the papers into his pocket, then stared down at himself. Sikes had hit him. Funny, he had never felt it. Only a shock, a numbness. Now Reed was coming back.

Catching up a sawed-off express shotgun, he started for the door, weaving like a drunken man. He never even got to the door.

The sound of galloping horses was all he could hear—galloping horses, and then a faint smell of something that reminded him of a time he had been wounded in North Africa. His eyes flickered open, and the first thing he saw was a room's wall with the picture of a man with mutton-chop whiskers and spectacles.

He turned his head and saw Jenny Curtin watching him. "So? You've decided to wake up. You're getting lazy, Matt. Mister Sabre. On the ranch you always were the first one up."

He stared at her. She had never looked half so charming, and that was bad. It was bad because it was time to be out of here and on a horse.

"How long have I been here?"

"Only about a day and a half. You lost a lot of blood."

"What happened at the ranch? Did Keys get there in time?"

"Yes, and I stayed. The others left right away."

"You stayed?"

"The others," she said quietly, "went down the road about two miles. There were Camp Gordon, Tom Judson, Pepito, and Keys. And Rado, of course. They went down the road while I stood out in the ranch yard and let them see me. The boys ambushed them."

"Was it much of a fight?"

"None at all. The surprise was so great that they broke and ran. Only three weren't able, and four were badly wounded."

"You found the papers? Including the one about McCarran sending the five thousand in marked bills to El Paso?"

"Yes," she said simply. "We found that. He planned on having Billy arrested and charged with theft. He planned that, and then, if he got killed, so much the better. It was only you he didn't count on."

"No." Matt Sabre stared at his hands, strangely white now. "He didn't count on me."

So it was all over now. She had her ranch, she was a free woman, and people would leave her alone. There was only one thing left. He had to tell her. To tell her that he was the one who had killed her husband.

He turned his head on the pillow. "One thing more," he began. "I . . ."

"Not now. You need rest."

"Wait. I have to tell you this. It's about . . . about Billy."

"You mean that you . . . you were the one who . . . ?"

"Yes, I . . ." He hesitated, reluctant at last to say it.

"I know. I know you did, Matt. I've known from the beginning, even without all the things you said."

"I talked when I was delirious?"

"A little. But I knew, Matt. Call it intuition, anything you like, but I knew. You see, you told me how his eyes were when he was drawing his gun. Who could have known that but the man who shot him?"

"I see." His face was white. "Then I'd better rest. I've got some traveling to do."

She was standing beside him. "Traveling? Do you have to go on, Matt? From all you said last night, I thought . . . I thought"—her face flushed—"maybe you . . . didn't want to travel any more. Stay with us, Matt, if you want to. We would like to have you, and Billy's been asking for you. He wants to know where his spurs are."

After a while, he admitted carefully: "Well, I

guess I should stay and see that he gets them. A fellow should always make good on his promises to kids, I reckon."

"You'll stay, then? You won't leave?"

Matt stared up at her. "I reckon," he said quietly, "I'll never leave unless you send me away."

She smiled and touched his hair. "Then you'll be here a long time, Mathurin Sabre . . . a very long time."

RIDERS OF THE DAWN

I

I rode down from the high blue hills and across the brush flats into Hattan's Point, a raw bit of spawning hell, scattered hit or miss along the rocky slope of a rust-topped mesa. Ah, it's a grand feeling to be young and tough with a heart full of hell, strong muscles, and quick, flexible hands! And the feeling that somewhere in town there's a man who would like to tear down your meat house with hands or gun.

It was like that, Hattan's Point was, when I swung down from my buckskin and gave him a word to wait with. A new town, a new challenge, and, if there were those who wished to take me on, let them come and be damned.

I knew the whiskey of this town would be the raw whiskey of the last town, and of the towns behind it, but I shoved through the batwing doors and downed a shot of rye and looked around, measuring the men along the bar and at the tables. None of these men did I know, yet I had seen them all before in a dozen towns. The big, hard-eyed rancher with the iron-gray hair who thought he was the bull of the woods, and the knife-like man beside him with the careful eyes who would be gun slick and fast as a striking snake. The big man turned his head toward me, as a great brown bear turns to look at something he could squeeze to nothing, if he wished.

"Who sent for you?"

There was harsh challenge in the words. The cold demand of a conqueror, and I laughed within me.

"Nobody sent for me. I ride where I want and stop when I want."

He was a man grown used to smaller men who spoke softly to him, and my answer was irritating.

"Then ride on," he said, "for you're not wanted in Hattan's Point."

"Sorry, friend," I said. "I like it here. I'm staying, and maybe, in whatever game you're playing, I'll buy chips. I don't like being ordered around by big frogs in such small puddles."

His big face flamed crimson, but before he could answer, another man spoke up, a tall young man with white hair.

"What he means is that there's trouble here, and men are taking sides. Those who stand upon neither side are everybody's enemy in Hattan's Point."

"So?" I smiled at them all, but my eyes held to the big bull of the woods. "Then maybe I'll choose a side. I always did like a fight."

"Then be sure you choose the right one"—this was from the knife-like man beside the bull—"and talk to me before you decide."

"I'll talk to you," I said, "or any man. I'm reasonable enough. But get this, the side I choose will be the right one."

The sun was bright on the street and I walked outside, feeling the warmth of it, feeling the cold from my muscles. Within me I chuckled, because I knew what they were saying back there. I'd thrown my challenge at them for pure fun; I didn't care about anyone. And then suddenly I did.

She stood on the boardwalk straight before me, slim, tall, with a softly curved body and magnificent eyes and hair of deepest black. Her skin was lightly tanned, her eyes an amazing green, her lips full and rich.

My black leather chaps were dusty, and my gray shirt was sweat-stained from the road. My jaws were lean and unshaven, and under my black, flat-crowned hat my hair was black and rumpled. I was in no shape to meet a girl like that, but there she was, the woman I wanted, my woman.

In two steps, I was beside her. "I realize," I said as she turned to face me, "the time is inopportune. My presence scarcely inspires interest, let alone affection and love, but this seemed the best time for you to meet the man you are to marry. The name is Mathurin Sabre. Furthermore, I might as well tell you now, I am of Irish and French extraction, have no money,

91

no property but a horse and the guns I wear, but I have been looking for you for years, and I could not wait to tell you that I was here, your future mate and husband." I bowed, hat in hand.

She stared, startled, amazed, and then angry. "Well, of all the egotistical . . ."

"Ah." My expression was one of relief. "Those are kind words, darling, wonderful words. More true romances have begun with those words than any other. And now, if you'll excuse me?"

Taking one step back, I turned, vaulted over the hitching rail, and untied my buckskin. Swinging into the saddle, I looked back. She was standing there, staring at me, her eyes wide, and the anger was leaving them.

"Good afternoon," I said, bowing again. "I'll call upon you later."

It was time to get out and away, but I felt good about it. Had I attempted to advance the acquaintance, I should have gotten nowhere, but my quick leaving would arouse her curiosity. There is no trait women possess more fortunate for men than their curiosity.

The livery stable at Hattan's Point was a huge and rambling structure that sprawled lazily over a corner at the beginning of the town. From a bin, I got a scoop of corn, and, while the buckskin absorbed this warning against hard days to come, I curried him carefully. A jingle of spurs warned me, and, when I looked around, a tall, very thin man was leaning against the stall post, watching me.

When I straightened up, I was looking into a pair of piercing dark eyes from under shaggy brows that seemed to overhang the long hatchet face. He was shabby and unkempt, but he wore two guns, the only man in town who I'd seen wearing two except for the knife-like man in the saloon.

"Hear you had a run in with Rud Maclaren."

"Run in? I'd not call it that. He suggested the country was crowded, and that I move on. So I told him I liked it here, and, if the fight looked good, I might choose a side."

"Good. Then I come right on time. Folks are talkin' about you. They say Canaval offered you a job on Maclaren's Bar M. Well, I'm beatin' him to it. I'm Jim Pinder, ramroddin' the CP outfit. I'll pay warrior wages, seventy a month an' found. All the ammunition you can use."

My eyes had strayed beyond him to two men lurking in a dark stall. They had, I was sure, come in with Pinder. The idea did not appeal to me. Shoving Pinder aside, I sprang into the middle of the open space between the rows of stalls.

"You two!" My voice rang in the echoing emptiness of the building. "Get out in the open! Start now or start shooting!"

My hands were wide, fingers spread, and right

then it did not matter to me what way they came. There was that old jumping devil in me, and the fury was driving me as it always did when action began to build up. Men who lurked in dark stalls did not appeal to me, or the men who hired them.

They came out slowly, hands wide. One of them was a big man with black hair and unshaven jowls. He looked surly. The other had the cruel, flat face of an Apache.

"Suppose I'd come shootin'?" the black-haired man sneered.

"Then they'd be planting you at sundown." My eyes held him. "If you don't believe that, cut loose your wolf right now."

That stopped him. He didn't like it, for they didn't know me and I was too ready. Wise enough to see that I was no half-baked gunfighter, they didn't know how much of it I could back up and weren't anxious to find out.

"You move fast." Pinder was staring at me with small eyes. "Suppose I had cut myself in with Blacky and the 'Pache?"

My chuckle angered him. "You? I had that pegged, Jim Pinder. When my guns came out, you would have died first. You're faster than either of those two, so you'd take yours first. Then Blacky, and after him"—I nodded toward the Apache—"him. He would be the hardest to kill."

Pinder didn't like it, and he didn't like me.

"I made an offer," he said.

"And you brought these coyotes to give me a rough time if I didn't take it? Be damned to you, Pinder! You can take your CP outfit and go to blazes!"

His lips thinned down and he stared at me. I've seldom seen such hatred in a man's eyes. "Then get out!" he said. "Get out fast! Join Maclaren, an' you die!"

"Then why wait? I'm not joining Maclaren so far as I know now, but I'm staying, Pinder. Any time you want what I've got, come shooting. I'll be ready."

"You swing a wide loop for a stranger. You started in the wrong country. You won't live long."

"No?" I gave it to him flat and face up on the table. "No? Well, I've a hunch I'll handle the shovel that throws dirt on your grave, and maybe trigger the gun that puts you there. I'm not asking for trouble, but I like it, so whenever you're ready, let me know."

With that I left them. Up the street there was a sign:

MOTHER O'HARA'S COOKING
MEALS FOUR BITS

With the gnawing appetite of me, that looked as likely a direction as any. It was early for supper, and there were few at table. The young man with white hair and the girl I loved, and a few scattered others who ate sourly and in silence.

When I shoved the door open and stood there with my hat shoved back on my head and a smile on my face, the girl looked up, surprised, but ready for battle. I grinned at her, and bowed. "How do you do, the future Missus Sabre? The pleasure of seeing you again so soon is unexpected, but real."

The man with her looked surprised, and the buxom woman of forty-five or so who came in from the kitchen looked quickly from one to the other of us.

The girl ignored me, but the man with the white hair nodded. "You've met Miss Maclaren, then?"

So? Maclaren it was? I might have suspected as much. "No, not formally. But we met briefly on the street, and I've been dreaming of her for years. It gives me great wonder to find her here, although when I see the food on the table, I don't doubt why she is so lovely if it is here she eats."

Mother O'Hara liked that. "Sure 'n' I smell the blarney in that," she said sharply. "But sit down, if you'd eat."

My hat came off, and I sat on the bench opposite my girl, who looked at her plate in cold silence.

"My name is Key Chapin." The white-haired

96

man extended his hand. "Yours, I take it, is Sabre?"

"Matt Sabre," I said.

A grizzled man from the foot of the table looked up. "Matt Sabre from Dodge, once marshal of Mobeetie, the Mogollon gunfighter?"

They all looked from him to me, and I accepted the cup of coffee Mother O'Hara poured.

"The gentleman knows me," I said quietly. "I've been known in those places."

"You refused Maclaren's offer?" Chapin asked.

"Yes, and Pinder's, too."

"Pinder?" Chapin's eyes were wary. "Is he in town?"

"Big as life." I could feel the girl's eyes on me. "Tell me what this fight is about?"

"What are most range wars about? Water, sheep, or grass. This one is water. There's a long valley east of here called Cottonwood Wash, and running east out of it is a smaller valley or cañon called the Two Bar. On the Two Bar is a stream of year-round water with volume enough to irrigate land or water thousands of cattle. Maclaren wants that water. The CP wants it."

"Who's got it?"

"A man named Ball. He's no fighter and has no money to hire fighters, but he hates Maclaren and refuses to do business with Pinder. So there they sit with the pot boiling and the lid about to blow off."

"And our friend Ball is right smack in the middle."

"Right. Gamblers around town are offering odds he won't last thirty days, even money that he'll be dead within ten."

That was enough for now. My eyes turned to the daughter of Rud Maclaren. "You can be buying your trousseau, then," I said, "for the time will not be long."

She looked at me coolly, but behind it there was a touch of impudence. "I'll not worry about it," she said calmly. "There're no weddings in Boot Hill."

They laughed at that, yet behind it I knew there was the feeling that she was right, and yet the something in me that was me told me no, it was not my time to go. Not by gun or horse or rolling river—not yet.

"You've put your tongue to prophecy, darling," I said, "and I'll not say that I'll not end in Boot Hill, where many another a good man has gone, but I will say this, and you sleep on it, daughter of Maclaren, for it's a bit of the truth. Before I sleep in Boot Hill, there'll be sons and daughters of yours and mine on this ground. Yes, and believe me"—I got up to go—"when my time comes, I'll be carried there by six tall sons of ours, and there'll be daughters of ours who'll weep at my grave, and you with them, remembering the years we've had."

When the door slapped shut behind me, there was silence inside, and then through the thin walls I heard Mother O'Hara speak.

"You'd better be buyin' that trousseau, Olga Maclaren, for there's a lad as knows his mind!"

This was the way of it then, and now I had planning to do, and my way to make in the world, for although I'd traveled wide and far, in many lands not my own, I'd no money or home to take her to. Behind me were wars and struggles, hunger, thirst, and cold, and the deep, splendid bitterness of fighting for a cause I scarcely understood, because there was in me the undying love of a lost cause and a world to win. And now I'd my own to win, and a threshold to find to carry her over.

And then, as a slow night wind moved upon my cheek and stirred the hair above my brow, I found an answer. I knew what I would do, and the very challenge of it sent my blood leaping, and the laughter came from my lips as I stepped into the street and started across it.

Then I stopped, for there was a man before me. He was a big man, towering above my six feet and two inches, broader and thicker than my two hundred pounds. He was a big-boned man and full of raw power, unbroken and brutal. He stood there, wide-legged before me, his face as wide as my two hands, his big head topped by a mat of tight curls, his hat missing somewhere.

"You're Sabre?" he said.

"Why, yes," I said, and he hit me.

Never did I see the blow start. Never even did I see the balled fist of his, but it bludgeoned my jaw like an axe butt, and something seemed to slam me behind the knees, and I felt myself going. He caught me again before I could fall, and then dropped astride of me and began to swing short, brutal blows to my head with both big fists. All of two hundred sixty pounds he must have weighed, and none of it wasted by fat. He was naked, raw, unbridled power.

Groggy, bloody, beaten, I fought to get up, but he was astride me, and my arms were pinned to my sides by his great knees. His fists were slugging me with casual brutality. Then, suddenly, he got up and stepped back and kicked me in the ribs.

"If you're conscious," he said, "hear me. I'm Morgan Park, and I'm the man who marries Olga Maclaren!"

My lips were swollen and bloody. "You lie!" I said, and he kicked me again, then stepped over me and walked away, whistling.

Somehow, I got my arms under me. Somehow, I dragged myself against the stage station wall, and then I lay there, my head throbbing like a great drum, the blood slowly drying on my split lips and broken face. It had been a beating I'd taken, and the marvel of it was with me. I'd not

100

been licked since I was a lad, and never in all my days had I felt such blows as these. His fists were like knots of oak, and the arms behind them like the limbs of a tree.

I had a broken rib, I thought, but one thing I knew. It was time for me to travel. Never would I have the daughter of Maclaren see me like this!

My hands found the building corner and I pulled myself to my feet, and, staggering behind the buildings, I got to the corner of the livery stable. Entering, I got to my horse, and, somehow, I got the saddle on him and led him out of the door. And then I stopped for an instant in the light.

Across the way, on the stoop of Mother O'Hara's, was Olga Maclaren!

The light was on my face, swollen, bloody, and broken. She stepped down off the porch and came over to me, looking up, her eyes wide with wonder. "So it's you. He found you then. He always hears, and this always happens. You see, it is not so simple a thing to marry Olga Maclaren." There seemed almost regret in her voice. "And now you're leaving."

"Leaving? That I am, but I'll be back!" The words fumbled through my swollen lips. "Have your trousseau ready, daughter of Maclaren. I mean what I say. Wait for me. I'll be coming again, darling, and, when I do, it will be first to tear down Morgan Park's great hulk, to rip him with my fists."

There was coolness in her voice, shaded with contempt. "You boast! All you have done is talk . . . and taken a beating!"

That made me grin, and the effort made me wince, but I looked down at her.

"It's a bad beginning at that, isn't it? But wait for me, darling, I'll be coming back."

I could feel her watching me ride down the street.

II

Throughout the night I rode into wilder and wilder country, always with the thought of what faced me. At daybreak, I bedded down in a cañon tall with pines, resting there while my side began to mend. My thoughts returned again and again to the shocking power of those punches I had taken. It was true the man had slugged me unexpectedly, and once pinned down I'd had no chance against his great weight. Nonetheless, I'd been whipped soundly. Within me there was a gnawing eagerness to go back—and not with guns. This man I must whip with my hands.

The Two Bar was the key to the situation. Could it be had with a gun and some blarney? The beating I'd taken rankled, and the contempt of Olga Maclaren, and with it the memory of the hatred of Jim Pinder and the coldness of Rud Maclaren. On the morning of the third day I mounted the buckskin and turned him toward the Two Bar.

A noontime sun was darkening my buckskin with sweat when I turned up Cottonwood Wash. There was green grass here, and trees, and the water that trickled down was clear and pure. The walls of the wash were high and the trees towered to equal them, and the occasional cattle looked fat and lazy, far better than elsewhere on this range. The path ended abruptly in a gate bearing a large sign in white letters against a black background.

TWO BAR GATE
RANGED FOR A SPENCER .56
SHOOTING GOING ON HERE

Ball evidently had his own ideas. No trespasser who got a bullet could say he hadn't been warned. Beyond this gate a man took his own chances. Taking off my hat, I rose in my stirrups and waved it toward the house.

A gun boomed, and I heard the sharp whap of a bullet whipping past. It was a warning shot, so I merely waved once more. That time the bullet was close, so I grabbed my chest with both hands and slid from the saddle to the ground. Speaking to the buckskin, I rolled over behind a boulder. Leaving my hat on the ground in plain sight, I removed a boot and placed it to be seen from the gate. Then I crawled into the brush, from where I could cover the gate.

Several minutes later, Ball appeared. Without coming through the gate, he couldn't see the boot was empty. He was a tall old man with a white handlebar mustache and shrewd eyes. No fool, he studied the layout carefully, but to all appearances his aim had miscalculated and scored a hit. He glanced at the strange brand on the buckskin and at the California bridle and bit. Finally, he opened the gate and came out, and, as he moved toward my horse, his back turned toward me.

"Freeze, Ball! You're dead in my sights!"

He stood still. "Who are you?" he finally demanded. "What you want with me?"

"No trouble. I came to talk business."

"I got no business with anybody."

"You've business with me. I'm Matt Sabre. I've had a run in with Jim Pinder and told off Maclaren when he told me to leave. I've taken a beating from Morgan Park."

Ball chuckled. "You say you want no trouble with me, but, from what you say, you've had it with ever'body else."

He turned at my word, and I holstered my gun. He stepped back far enough to see the boot, then he grinned. "Good trick. I'll not bite on that one again. What you want?"

Pulling on my boot and retrieving my hat, I told him. "I've no money. I'm a fighting man and a sucker for the tough side of any scrap. When I rode into Hattan's Point, I figured on trouble, but when I saw Olga Maclaren, I decided to stay and marry her. I've told her so."

"No wonder Park beat you. He's run off the local lads." He studied me curiously. "What did she say?"

"Very little, and, when I told her I was coming back to face Park again, she thought I was loud-mouthed."

"Aim to try him again?"

"I'm going to whip him. But that's not all. I plan to stay in this country, and there's only one ranch in this country I want or would have."

Ball's lips thinned. "This one?"

"It's the best, and anybody who owns it stands in the middle of trouble. I'd be mighty uncomfortable anywhere else."

"What you aim to do about me? This here's my ranch."

"Let's walk up to your place and talk it over."

"We'll talk here." Ball's hands were on his hips and I had no doubt he'd go for a gun if I made a wrong move. "Speak your piece."

"All right. Here it is. You're bucking a stacked deck. Gamblers are offering thirty to one you won't last thirty days. Both Maclaren and Pinder are out to get you. What I want is a fighting, working partnership. Or you sell out and I'll pay you when I can. I'll take over the fight."

He nodded toward the house. "Come on up. We'll talk this over."

Two hours later the deal was ironed out. He could not stay awake every night. He could not work and guard his stock. He could not go to town for supplies. Together we could do all of it.

"You'll be lucky if you last a week," he told me. "When they find out, they'll be fit to be tied."

"They won't find out right away. First, I'll buy supplies and ammunition, and get back here."

"Good idea. But leave Morgan Park alone. He's as handy with a gun as his fists."

The Two Bar controlled most of Cottonwood Wash and on its eastern side opened into the desert wilderness with only occasional patches of grass and much desert growth. Maclaren's Bar M and Pinder's CP bordered the ranch on the west, with Maclaren's range extending to the desert land in one portion, but largely west of the Two Bar.

Both ranches had pushed the Two Bar cattle back, usurping the range for their own use. In the process of pushing them north, most of the Two Bar calves had vanished under Bar M or CP brands.

"Mostly the CP," Ball advised. "Them Pinders are pizen mean. Rollie rode with the James boys a few times, and both of them were with Quantrill. Jim's a fast gun, but nothin' to compare with Rollie."

At daylight, with three unbranded mules to carry the supplies, I started for Hattan's Point, circling around to hit the trail on the side away from the Two Bar. The town was quiet enough, and the day warm and still. As I loaded the supplies, I was sweating. The sweat trickled into my eyes and my side pained me. My face was still puffed, but both my eyes were now open. Leading my mules out of town, I concealed them in some brush with plenty of grass, and then returned to Mother O'Hara's.

Key Chapin and Canaval were there, and Canaval looked up at me. "Had trouble?" he asked. "That job at the Bar M is still open."

"Thanks. I'm going to run my own outfit." Foolish though it was, I said it. Olga had come in the door behind me, her perfume told me who it was, and even without it something in my blood would have told me. From that day on she was never to be close to me without my knowledge. It was something deep and exciting that was between us.

"Your own outfit?" They were surprised. "You're turning nester?"

"No. Ranching." Turning, I swept off my

hat and indicated the seat beside me. "Miss Maclaren? May I have the pleasure?"

Her green eyes were level and measuring. She hesitated, then shook her head. Walking around the table, she seated herself beside Canaval.

Chapin was puzzled. "You're ranching? If there's any open range around here, I don't know of it."

"It's a place over east of here," I replied lightly. "The Two Bar."

"What about the Two Bar?" Rud Maclaren had come in. He stood, cold and solid, staring down at me.

Olga glanced up at her father, some irony in her eyes. "Mister Sabre was telling us that he is ranching . . . on the Two Bar."

"What?" Glasses and cups jumped at his voice, and Mother O'Hara hurried in from her kitchen, rolling pin in hand.

"That's right." I was enjoying it. "I've a working partnership with Ball. He needed help, and I didn't want to leave despite all the invitations I was getting." Then I added: "A man dislikes being far from the girl he's to marry."

"What's that?" Maclaren demanded, his eyes puzzled.

"Why, Father"—Olga's eyes widened—"haven't you heard? The whole town is talking of it. Mister Sabre has said he is going to marry me."

"I'll see him in hell first," Maclaren replied flatly. "Young man, you stop using my daughter's name or you'll face me."

"No one," I said quietly, "has more respect for your daughter's name than I. It's true that I've said she was to be my wife. That is not disrespectful, and it's certainly true. As for facing you, I'd rather not. I'd like to keep peace with my future father-in-law."

Canaval chuckled and even Olga seemed amused. Key Chapin looked up at Rud. "One aspect of this may have escaped you. Sabre is now a partner of Ball. Why not make it easy for Sabre to stay on, then buy him out?"

Maclaren's head lifted as he absorbed the idea. He looked at Sabre with new interest. "We might do business, young man."

"We might," I replied, "but not under threats. Nor do I intend to sell out my partner. Nor did I take the partnership with any idea of selling out. Tomorrow or the next day I shall choose a building site. Also, I expect to restock the Two Bar range. All of which brings me to the point of this discussion. It has come to my attention that Bar M cattle are trespassing on Two Bar range. You have just one week to remove them. The same goes for the CP. You've been told and you understand. I hope we'll have no further trouble."

Maclaren's face purpled with fury. Before he could find words to reply, I was on my feet. "It's been nice seeing you," I told Olga. "If you care to help plan your future home, why don't you ride over?"

With that, I stepped out the door before Maclaren could speak. Circling the building, I headed for my horse.

Pinder's black-haired man was standing there with a gun in his hand. Hatred glared from his eyes.

"Figured you pulled a smart one, hey?" he sneered. "Now I'll kill you!"

His finger started to whiten with pressure, and I hurled myself aside and palmed my gun. Even before I could think, my gun jarred in my hand. Once. Twice.

Blacky's bullet had torn my shirt collar and left a trace of blood on my neck. Blacky stared at me, then lifted to his toes and fell, measuring his length upon the hard ground.

Men rushed from the buildings, crowding around. "Seen it," one man explained quietly. "Blacky laid for him with a drawed gun."

Canaval was among the men. He looked at me with cool, attentive gaze. "A drawn gun? That was fast, man."

Ball was at the gate when I arrived. "Trouble?" he asked quickly.

My account was brief. "Well, one less for later," said Ball. "If it had to be anybody, it's better it was Blacky, but now the Pinders will be after you."

"Where does Morgan Park stand?" I asked. "And what about Key Chapin?"

"Park?" Ball said. "He's fixin' to marry the Maclaren girl. That's where his bread's buttered. He's got him a ranch on the Arizona line, but he don't stay there much. Chapin publishes the *Rider's Voice*, a better newspaper'n you'd expect in this country. He's also a lawyer, plays a good hand of poker, an' never carries a gun. If anybody isn't takin' sides, it's him."

Mostly I considered the cattle situation. Our calves had been rustled by the large outfits, and, if we were to prosper, we must get rid of the stock we now had and get some young stuff. Our cattle would never be in better shape, and would get older and tougher. Now was the time to sell. A drive was impossible, for two of us couldn't be away at once, and nobody wanted any part of a job with the Two Bar. Ball was frankly discouraged.

"No use, Matt. They got us bottled up. We're through whenever they want to take us."

An idea occurred to me. "By the way, when I was drifting down around Organ Rock the other day, I spotted an outfit down there in the hills. Know 'em?"

Ball's head came up sharply. "Should have warned you. Stay away. That's the Benaras place, the B Bar B brand. There's six in the family that I know of, an' they have no truck with anybody. Dead shots, all of 'em. Few years back some rustlers run off some of their stock. Nobody heard no more about it until Sheriff Will Tharp was back in the badlands east of here. He hadn't seen hide nor hair of man nor beast for miles when suddenly he comes on six skeletons hanging from a rock tower."

"Skeletons?"

Ball took the pipe from his mouth and spat. "Six of 'em, an' a sign hung to 'em readin' . . . 'They rustled B Bar B cows.' Nothin' more."

But quite enough! The Benaras outfit had been let strictly alone after that. Nevertheless, an idea was in my mind, and the very next morning I saddled up and drifted south.

It was wild and lonely country, furrowed and eroded by thousands of years of sun, wind, and rain. A country tumbled and broken as if by an insane giant. Miles of raw, unfleshed land with only occasional spots of green to break its everlasting reds, pinks, and whites. Like an oasis, there appeared a sudden cluster of trees, green fields, and fat, drifting cattle. "Whoever these folks are, Buck," I commented to my horse, "they work hard."

The click of a drawn-back hammer froze Buck in his tracks, and carefully I kept my hands on the saddle horn. "Goin' somewhar, stranger?"

Nobody was in sight among the boulders at the edge of the field.

"Yes. I'm looking for the boss of the B Bar B."

"What might you want with him?"

"Business talk. I'm friendly."

The chuckle was dry. "Ever see a man covered by two Spencers that wasn't friendly?"

The next was a girl's voice. "Who you ridin' for?"

"I'm Matt Sabre, half owner of the Two Bar, Ball's outfit."

"You mean that ol' coot took a partner? You could be lyin'."

"Do I see the boss?"

"I reckon." A tall boy of eighteen stepped from the rocks. Lean and drawn, his hatchet face looked tough and wise. He carried his Spencer as if it was part of him. He motioned with his head.

The old man of the tribe was standing in front of a house built like a fort. Tall as his son, he was straight as a lodgepole pine. He looked me up and down, then said: "Get down an' set." And then they went inside.

A stout motherly woman put out some cups and poured coffee. Explaining who I was, I said: "We've some fat stock about ready to drive. I'd like to make a swap for some of your young stuff. We can't make a drive, don't dare even leave the place or they'd steal it from us. Our stock is in good shape, but all our young stuff has been rustled."

"You're talkin'." He studied me from under shaggy brows. He looked like a patriarch right out of the Bible, a hard-bitten old man of the tribe who knew his own mind and how to make it stick. He listened as I explained our set-up and our plans. Finally, he nodded. "All right, Sabre. We'll swap. My boys will help you drive 'em back here."

"No need for that. Once started down the cañons, I'll need no help. No use you getting involved in this fight."

He turned his fierce blue eyes on me. "I'm buyin' cows," he said grimly. "Anybody who wants trouble over that, let 'em start it!"

"Now, Paw!" Mother Benaras smiled at me. "Paw figures he's still a-feudin'."

Old Bob Benaras knocked out his pipe on the hearth. "We're beholden to no man, nor will we backwater for any man. Nick, roust out an' get Zeb, then saddle up an' ride with this man. You ride to this man's orders. Start no trouble, but back up for nobody. Understand?" He looked around at me. "You'll eat first. Maw, set up the table. We've a guest in the house." He looked searchingly at me. "Had any trouble with Jim Pinder yet?"

It made a short tale, then I added: "Blacky braced me in town a few days ago. Laid for me with a drawn gun."

Benaras stared at me and the boys exchanged looks. The old roan tamped tobacco into his pipe. "He had it comin'. Jolly had trouble with that one. Figured soon or late he'd have to kill him. Glad you done it."

All the way back to the Two Bar we watched the country warily, but it was not until we were coming up to the gate that anyone was sighted. Two riders were on the lip of the wash, staring at us through a glass. We passed through the gate and started up the trail. There was no challenge.

Nick said suddenly: "I smell smoke!"

Fear went through me like an electric shock. Slapping the spurs to my tired buckskin, I put the horse up the trail at a dead run, Nick and Zeb right behind me. Turning the bend in the steep trail, I heard the crackle of flames and saw the ruins of the house!

All was in ruins, the barn gone, the house a sagging, blazing heap. Leaving my horse on the run, I dashed around the house. "Ball!" I yelled. "Ball!" And above the crackle of flames, I heard a cry.

He was back in a niche of rock near the spring. How he had lived this long I could not guess. His clothes were charred and it was obvious he had somehow crawled, wounded, from the burning house. He had been fairly riddled with bullets.

His fierce old eyes were pleading. "Don't let 'em git . . . git the place. Yours . . . it's yours now." His eyes went to Nick and Zeb. "You're witnesses. I leave it to him. Never to sell . . . never to give up!"

"Who was it?" For the first time in my life I really wanted to kill. Although I had known this old man for only a few days, I had come to feel affection for him, and respect. Now he was dying, shot down and left for dead in a blazing house.

"Pinder." His voice was hoarse. "Jim an' Rollie. Rollie, he . . . he was dressed like you. Never had no chance. Fun- . . . funny thing. I . . . I thought I saw . . . Park."

"Morgan Park?" I was incredulous. "With the Pinders?"

His lips stirred, but he died forming the words. When I got up, there was in me such hatred as I had never believed was possible. "Every one of them!" I said. "I'll kill every man of them for this!"

"Amen!" Zeb and Nick spoke as one. "He was a good man. Pappy liked him."

"Did you hear him say Morgan Park was with the Pinders?"

"Sounded like it," Zeb admitted, "but 'tain't reasonable. He's thick with the Maclarens. Couldn't have been him."

Zeb was probably right. The light had been bad, and Ball had been wounded. He could have made a mistake.

The stars went out and night moved in over the hills and gathered black and rich in the cañons. Standing there in the darkness we could smell the smoke from the burned house and see occasional sparks and flickers of tiny flames among the charred timbers. A ranch had been given me, but I had lost a friend. The road before me stretched dark and long, a road I must walk alone, gun in hand.

III

For two days, we combed the draws and gathered cattle, yet at the end of the second day we had but three hundred head. The herds of the Two Bar had been sadly depleted by the rustling of the big brands. On the morning of the third day we started the herd. Neither of the men had questioned me, but now Zeb wanted to know: "You aim to leave the ranch unguarded? Ain't you afraid they'll move in?"

"If they do, they can move out or be buried here. That ranch was never to be given up, and, believe me, it won't be!"

The cañon channeled the drive and the cattle were fat and easy to handle. It took us all day to make the drive, but my side pained me almost none at all, and only that gnawing fury at the killers of the old man remained to disturb me.

They had left the wounded man to burn, and for that they would pay.

Jonathan and Jolly Benaras helped me take the herd of young stuff back up the trail. Benaras had given me at least fifty head more than I had asked, but the cattle I had turned over to him were as good as money in the bank, so he lost nothing by his generosity.

When we had told him what had happened, he had nodded. "Jolly was over to Hattan's Point. It was the Pinders, all right. That Apache tracker of theirs along with Bunt Wilson and Corby Kitchen an' three others. They were with the Pinders."

"Hear anything about Morgan Park?"

"No. Some say Lyell, that rider of Park's, was in the crowd."

That could have been it. Ball might have meant to tell me it was a rider of Park's. We pushed the young stuff hard to get back, but Jonathan rode across the drag before we arrived.

"Folks at your place. Two, three of 'em."

My face set cold as stone. "Bring the herd. I'll ride ahead."

Jonathan's big Adam's apple bobbed. "Jolly an' me, we ain't had much fun lately. Cain't we ride with you?"

An idea hit me. "Where's their camp?"

"Foot of the hill where the house was. They got a tent."

"Then we'll take the herd. Drive 'em right over the tent!"

Jolly had come back to the drag. He chuckled. "Why, sure!" He grinned at Jonathan. "Won't Nick an' Zeb be sore? Missin' all the fun?"

We started the herd. They were young stuff and still full of ginger, ready enough to run. They came out of the cañon not more than four hundred yards from the camp and above the gate. Then we really turned them loose, shooting and shouting; we started that herd on a dead run for the camp. Up ahead we saw men springing to their feet, and one man raced for his rifle. They hadn't expected me to arrive with cattle, so they were caught completely off guard. Another man made a dive for his horse and the startled animal sprang aside, and, as he grabbed again, it kicked out with both hoofs and started to run.

Running full tilt, the herd hit the camp. The man who lost his horse scrambled atop a large rock and the others lit out for the cliffs, scattering away from the charging cattle. But the herd went through the camp, tearing up the tent, grinding the food into the earth, smearing the fire, and smashing the camp utensils into broken and useless things under their charging hoofs.

One of the men who had gotten into the saddle swung his horse and came charging back, his face red with fury. "What goes on here?" he yelled.

The horse was a Bar M. Maclaren's men had

beaten the CP to it. Kneeing my horse close to him, I said: "I'm Matt Sabre, owner of the Two Bar, with witnesses to prove it. You're trespassing. Now light a shuck!"

"I will like hell!" His face was dark with fury. "I got my orders, an' I . . ."

My fist smashed into his teeth and he left the saddle, hitting the ground with a thud. Blazing with fury, I lit astride him, jerking him to his feet. My left hooked hard to his jaw and my right smashed him in the wind. He went down, but he got up fast and came in swinging. He was a husky man, mad clear through, and for about two minutes we stood toe to toe and swapped it out. Then he started to back up and I caught him with a sweeping right that knocked him to the dust. He started to get up, then thought the better of it. "I'll kill you for this!"

"When you're ready," I said, then turned around. Jonathan and Jolly had rounded up two of the men, and they stood waiting for me. One was a slim, hard-faced youngster who looked like the devil was riding him. The other was a stocky redhead with a scar on his jaw.

The redhead stared at me, hatred in his eyes. "You ruined my outfit. What kind of a deal is this?"

"If you ride for a fighting brand, you take the good with the bad," I told him. "What did you expect when you came up here? A tea party? You go back and tell Maclaren not to send boys to do a man's job and that the next trespasser will be shot."

The younger one looked at me, sneering. "What if he sends me?" Contempt twisted his lips. "If I'd not lost my gun in the scramble, I'd make you eat that."

"Jolly. Lend me your gun."

Without a word, Jolly Benaras handed it to me.

The youngster's eyes were cold and calculating, but wary now. He suspected a trick, but could not guess what it might be.

Taking the gun by the barrel, I walked toward him. "You get your chance," I said. "I'm giving you this gun and you can use it any way you like. Try a border roll or shoot through that open-tip holster. Any way you try it, I'm going to kill you."

He stared at me, and then at the gun. His tongue touched his lips. He wanted that gun more than anything else in the world. He had guts, that youngster did, guts and the streak of viciousness it takes to make a killer, but suddenly he was face to face with it at close range and he didn't like it. He would learn, if he lived long enough, but right now he didn't like any part of it. Yet he wore the killer's brand and we both knew it.

"It's a trick," he said. "You ain't that much of a fool."

"Fool?" That brought my own fury surging

to the top. "Why, you cheap, phony would-be badman! I'd give you two guns and beat you any day you like! I'll face you right now. You shove your gun in my belly and I'll shove mine in yours! If you want to die, that makes it easy! Come on, gunslick! What do you say?"

Crazy? Right then I didn't care. His face turned whiter but his eyes were vicious. He was trembling with eagerness to grab that gun. But face to face? Guns shoved against the body? We would both die; we couldn't miss. He shook his head, his lips dry.

My fingers held the gun by the barrel. Tossing it up suddenly, I caught it by the butt, and without stopping the motion I slashed the barrel down over his skull, and he hit the dirt at my feet. Turning my back on them, I returned the pistol to Jolly.

"You!" I said then to the redhead. "Take off your boots!"

"Huh?" He was startled.

"Take 'em off! Then take his off! When he comes out of it, start walking!"

"Walkin'?" Red's face blanched. "Look, man, I'll . . ."

"You'll walk. All the way back to Hattan's Point or the Bar M. You'll start learnin' what it means to try stealin' a man's ranch."

"It was orders," he protested.

"You could quit, couldn't you?"

His face was sullen. "Wait until Maclaren hears of this! You won't last long! Far's that goes"—he motioned at the still figure on the ground—"he'll be huntin' you now. That's Bodie Miller!"

The name was familiar. Bodie Miller had killed five or six men. He was utterly vicious, and, although lacking seasoning, he had it in him to be one of the worst of the badmen.

We watched them start, three men in their sock feet with twenty miles of desert and mountains before them. Now they knew what they had tackled. They would know what war meant.

The cattle were no cause for worry. They would drift into cañons where there was plenty of grass and water, more than on the B Bar B.

"Sure you won't need help?" Jolly asked hopefully. "We'd like t'side you."

"Not now. This is my scrap."

They chuckled. "Well"—Jolly grinned—"they cain't never say you didn't walk in swingin'. You've jumped nearly the whole durned country!"

Nobody knew that better than I, so, when they were gone, I took my buckskin and rode back up the narrow Two Bar Cañon. It narrowed down and seemed to end, and, unless one knew, a glance up the cañon made it appear to be boxed in, but actually there was a turn and a narrower cañon leading into a maze of cañons and broken lava flows. There was an ancient cliff house back there, and in it Ball and I had stored supplies for a last-ditch stand. There was an old *kiva* with one side broken down and room enough to stable the buckskin.

At daybreak, I left the cañon behind me, riding watchfully, knowing I rode among enemies. No more than two miles from the cañon toward which I was heading, I rounded a bend and saw a dozen riders coming toward me at a canter. Sighting me, they yelled in chorus, and a shot rang out. Wheeling the buckskin, I slapped the spurs to him and went up the wash at a dead run. A bullet whined past my ear, but I dodged into a branch cañon and raced up a trail that led to the top of the plateau. Behind me, I heard the riders race past the cañon's mouth, then a shout as a rider glimpsed me, and the wheeling of horses as they turned. By the time they entered the cañon mouth, I was atop the mesa.

Sliding to the ground, Winchester in hand, I took a running dive to shelter among some rocks and snapped off a quick shot. A horse stumbled and his rider went over his head. I opened up, firing as rapidly as I could squeeze off the shots. They scattered for shelter, one man scrambling with a dragging leg.

Several of the horses had raced away, and a couple of others stood ground-hitched. On one of these was a big canteen. A bullet emptied it, and, when the other horse turned a few minutes later,

I shot into that canteen, also. Bullets ricocheted around me, but without exposing themselves they could not get a good shot at me, while I could cover their hide-out without trouble.

A foot showed and I triggered my rifle. A bit of leather flew up and the foot was withdrawn. My position could not have been better. As long as I remained where I was, they could neither advance nor retreat, but were pinned down and helpless. They were without water, and it promised to be an intensely hot day. Having no desire to kill them, I still wished to make them thoroughly sick of the fight. These men enjoyed the fighting as a break in the monotony of range work, but, knowing cowhands, I knew they would become heartily sick of a battle that meant waiting, heat, no water, and no chance to fight back.

For some time, all was still. Then a man tried to crawl back toward the cañon mouth, evidently believing himself unseen. Letting go a shot at a rock ahead of him, I splattered his face with splinters, and he ducked back, swearing loudly.

"Looks like a long hot day, boys!" I yelled. "See what it means when you jump a small outfit? Ain't so easy as you figured, is it?"

Somebody swore viciously and there were shouted threats. My own canteen was full, so I sat back and rolled a smoke. Nobody moved below, but the sun began to level its burning rays into the oven of the cañon mouth. The hours marched slowly by, and from time to time, when some thirsty soul grew restive at waiting, I threw a shot at him.

"How long you figure you can keep us here?" one of them yelled. "When we get out, we'll get you!"

"Maybe you won't get out!" I yelled back cheerfully. "I like it here! I've got water, shade, grub, and plenty of smokin' tobacco! Also," I added, "I've got better than two hundred rounds of ammunition! You *hombres* are riding for the wrong spread!"

Silence descended over the cañon and two o'clock passed. Knowing they could get no water aggravated thirst. The sun swam in a coppery sea of heat; the horizon lost itself in heat waves. Sweat trickled down my face and down my body under the arms. Where I lay, there was not only shade but a slight breeze, while down there heat would reflect from the cañon walls and all wind would be shut off. Finally, letting go with a shot, I slid back out of sight and got to my feet.

My buckskin cropped grass near some rocks, well under the shade. Shifting my rifle to my left hand, I slid down the bank, mopping my face with my right. Then I stopped stockstill, my right-hand belt high. Backed up against a rock near my horse was a man I knew at once although I had never seen him—Rollie Pinder.

"You gave them boys hell," he said conversationally, "an' good for 'em. They're Bar M riders. It's a shame it has to end."

"Yeah," I drawled, watching him closely. He could be waiting for only one reason.

"Hear you're mighty fast, but it won't do you any good. I'm Rollie Pinder."

As he spoke, he grabbed for his gun. My left hand was on the rifle barrel a few inches ahead of the trigger guard, the butt in front of me, the barrel pointed slightly up. I tilted the gun hard and the stock struck my hip as my hand slapped the trigger guard and trigger.

Rollie's gun had come up smoking, but my finger closed on the trigger a split second before his slug hit me. It felt as if I had been kicked in the side, and I took a staggering step back, a rock rolling under my foot just enough to throw me out of the line of his second shot. Then I fired again, having worked the lever unconsciously.

Rollie went back against the rocks and tried to bring his gun up. He fired as I did. The world weaved and waved before me, but Rollie was down on his face, great holes torn in his back where the .44 slugs had emerged. Turning, scarcely able to walk, I scrambled up the incline to my former position. My head was spinning and my eyes refused to focus, but the shots had startled the men and they were getting up. If they started after me now, I was through.

The ground seemed to dip and reel, but I got

off a shot, then another. One man went down, and the others vanished as if swallowed by the earth. Rolling over, my breath coming in ragged gasps, I ripped my shirt tail off and plugged cloth into my wounds. I had to get away at all costs, but I could never climb back up to the cliff house, even if the way were open.

My rifle dragging, I crawled and slid to the buckskin. Twice I almost fainted from weakness. Pain was gripping my vitals, squeezing and knotting them. Somehow, I got to my horse, grabbed a stirrup, managed to get a grip on the pommel, and pulled myself into the saddle. Getting my rifle back into its scabbard, I got some pigging strings and tied myself into the saddle. Then I started the buckskin toward the wilderness, and away from my enemies.

Day was shooting crimson arrows into the vast bowl of the sky when my eyes opened again. My head swam with effort, and I stared about, seeing nothing familiar. Buck had stopped beside a small spring in a cañon. There was grass and a few trees, with not far away the ruin of a rock house. On the sand beside the spring was the track of a mountain lion, several deep tracks and what might be a mountain sheep, but no cow, horse, or human tracks.

Fumbling with swollen fingers, I untied the pigging strings and slid to the ground. Buck snorted and side-stepped, then put his nose down to me inquiringly. He drew back from the smell of stale clothes and dried blood, and I lay there, staring up at him, a crumpled human thing, my body raw with pain and weakness. "It's all right, Buck," I whispered. "We'll pull through. We've got to pull through."

IV

Over me the sky's high gray faded to pink shot with blood-red swords that swept the red into gold. As the sun crept up, I lay there, still beneath the wide sky, my body washed by a sea of dull pain that throbbed and pulsed in my muscles and veins. Yet deep within beat a deeper, stronger pulse, the pulse of the fighting man that would not let me die without fighting, that would not let me lie long without movement.

Turning over, using hand grasps of grass, I pulled myself to the spring and drank deep of the cool, clear, life-giving water. The wetness of it seemed to creep through all my tissues, bringing peace to my aching muscles and life to my starved body. To live I must drink, and I must eat, and my body must have rest and time to mend. Over and over these thoughts went through my mind, and over and over I said them, staring at my helpless hands. With contempt I looked at them, hating them for their weakness. And then

I began to fight for life in those fingers, willing them to movement, to strength. Slowly my left hand began to stir, to lift at my command, to grasp a stick.

Triumph went through me. I was not defeated! Triumph lent me strength, and from this small victory I went on to another—a bit of broken manzanita placed across the first, a handful of scraped up leaves, more sticks. Soon I would have a fire.

I was a creature fighting for survival, wanting only to live and to fight. Through waves of delirium and weakness, I dragged myself to an aspen where I peeled bark for a vessel. Fainting there, coming to, struggling back to the place for my fire, putting the bark vessel together with clumsy fingers. With the bark vessel, a sort of box, I dipped into the water but had to drag it to the sand, lacking the strength to lift it up, almost crying with weakness and pain.

Lighting my fire, I watched the flames take hold. Then I got the bark vessel atop two rocks in the fire, and the flames rose around it. As long as the flames were below the water level of the vessel, I knew the bark would not burn, for the heat was absorbed by the water inside. Trying to push a stick under the vessel, I leaned too far and fainted.

When next I opened my eyes, the water was boiling. Pulling myself to a sitting position, I unbuckled my thick leather belt and let my guns fall back on the ground. Then carefully I opened my shirt and tore off a corner of it. I soaked it in the boiling water and began to bathe my wounds. Gingerly working the cloth plugs free of the wounds, I extracted them. The hot water felt good, but the sight of the wound in my side was frightening. It was red and inflamed, but near as I could see, as I bathed it, the bullet had gone through and touched nothing vital. The second slug had gone through the fleshy part of my thigh, and after bathing that wound, also, I lay still for a while, regaining strength and soaking up the heat.

Nearby there was patch of prickly pear, so I crawled to it and cut off a few big leaves, then I roasted them to get off the spines and bound the pulp against the wounds. Indians had used it to fight inflammations, and it might help. I found a clump of *amolilla* and dug some of the roots, scraping them into hot water. They foamed up when stirred and I drank the foamy water, remembering the Indians used the drink to carry off clotted blood, and a man's bullet wounds healed better after he drank it.

Then I made a meal of squaw cabbage and breadroot, not wanting to attempt getting at my saddlebags. Yet, when evening came and my fever returned, I managed to call Buck to me and loosen the girths. The saddle dropped, bringing with it my bedroll and saddlebags. Then I hobbled Buck and got the bridle off.

The effort exhausted me, so I crawled into my bedroll. My fever haunted the night with strange shapes, and guns seemed crashing about me. Men and darkness fought on the edge of my consciousness. Morgan Park—Jim Pinder—Rud Maclaren—and the sharply feral face of Bodie Miller.

The nuzzling of Buck awakened me in the cold light of day. "All right, Buck," I whispered. "I'm awake. I'm alive."

My weakness horrified me. If my enemies found me, they would not hesitate to kill me, and Buck must have left a trail easily followed. High up the cañon wall there was a patch of green, perhaps a break in the rock. Hiding my saddle under some brush, and taking with me my bedroll, saddlebags, rifle, and rope, I dragged myself toward an eyebrow of trail up the cliff.

If there was a hanging valley up there, it was just what I wanted. The buckskin wandered after me, more from curiosity than anything else. Getting atop a boulder, I managed to slide onto his back, then kneed him up the steep trail. A mountain horse, he went willingly, and in a few minutes we had emerged into a high hanging valley.

A great crack in the rock, it was flat-floored and high-walled, yet the grass was rich and green.

Somewhere water was running, and before me was a massive stone tower all of sixty feet high. Blackened by age and by fire, it stood beside a spring, quite obviously the same as that from which I had been drinking below. The hanging valley comprised not over three acres of land seemingly enclosed on the far side, and almost enclosed on the side where I had entered.

The ancient Indians who had built the tower had known a good thing when they saw it, for here was shelter and defense, grass, water, and many plants. Beside the tower some stunted maize, long since gone native, showed there had once been planting here. Nowhere was there any evidence that a human foot had trod here in centuries.

A week went slowly by, and nothing disturbed my camp. Able to walk a few halting steps, I explored the valley. The maize had been a fortunate discovery, for Indians had long used a mush made of the meal as an hourly application for bullet wounds. With this and other remedies my recovery became more rapid. The jerky gave out, but with snared rabbits and a couple of sage hens I managed. And then I killed a deer, and with the wild vegetables growing about I lived well.

Yet a devil of impatience was riding me. My ranch was in the hands of my enemies, and each day of absence made the chance of recovery grow less. Then, after two weeks, I was walking, keeping watch from a look-out spot atop the cliff and rapidly regaining strength. On the sixteenth day of my absence I decided to make an effort to return.

The land through which I rode was utterly amazing. Towering monoliths of stone, long, serrated cliffs of salmon-colored sandstone, and nothing human. It was almost noon of the following day before the buckskin's ears lifted suddenly. It took several seconds for me to discover what drew his attention, and then I detected a lone rider. An hour later, from a pinnacle of rock near a tiny seep of water, the rider was drawing near, carefully examining the ground.

A surge of joy went through me. It was Olga Maclaren.

Stepping out from the shadow, I waited for her to see me, and she did, almost at once. How I must look, I could guess. My shirt was heavy with dust, torn by a bullet and my own hands. My face was covered with beard and my cheeks drawn and hollow, but the expression on her face was only of relief.

"Matt?" Her voice was incredulous. "You're alive?"

"Did you think I'd die before we were married, daughter of Maclaren? Did you think I'd die before you had those sons I promised? Right now, I'm coming back to claim my own."

"Back?" The worry on her face was obvious. "You must never go back. You're believed dead, so you are safe. Go away while there's time."

"Did you think I'd run? Olga, I've been whipped by Morgan Park, shot by Rollie Pinder, and attacked by the others, but Pinder is dead, and Park's time is coming. No, I made a promise to a fine old man named Ball, another one to myself, and one to you, and I'll keep them all. In my time I've backed up, I've side-stepped, and occasionally I've run, but always to come back and fight again."

She looked at me, and some of the fear seemed to leave her. Then she shook her head. "But you can't go back now. Jim Pinder has the Two Bar."

"Then he'll move," I promised her.

Olga had swung down from her horse and lifted my canteen. "You've water!" she exclaimed. "They all said no man could survive out there in that waste, even if he was not wounded."

"You believed them?"

"No." She hesitated. "I knew you'd be alive somewhere."

"You know your man then, Olga Maclaren. Does it mean that you love me, too?"

She hesitated and her eyes searched mine, but when I would have moved toward her, she drew back, half frightened. Her lips parting a little, her breast lifting suddenly as she caught her breath. "It isn't time for that now . . . please!"

It stopped me, knowing what she said was true. "You are sure you weren't trailed?"

She shook her head. "I've been careful. Every day."

"This isn't the first day you looked for me?"

"Oh, no." She looked at me, her eyes shadowed with worry. "I was afraid you were lying somewhere, bloody and suffering." Her eyes studied me, noting the torn shirt, the pallor of my face. "And you have been."

"Rollie was good. He was very good."

"Then it was you who killed him?"

"Who else?"

"Canaval and Bodie Miller found him after they realized you were gone from the mesa where you pinned them down. Canaval was sure it had been you, but some of them thought it was the mountain boys."

"They've done no fighting for me although they wanted to. You'd best start back. I've work to do."

"But you're in no shape! You're sick!" She stared at me.

"I can still fight," I said. "Tell your father you've seen me. Tell him the Two Bar was given me in the presence of witnesses. Tell him his stock is to be off that range . . . at once!"

"You forget that I am my father's daughter."

"And my future wife."

"I've promised no such thing!" she flared. "You

136

know I'd never marry you! I'll admit you're attractive, and you're a devil, but marry you? I'd die first!"

Her breast heaved and her eyes flashed and I laughed at her. "Tell your father, though, and ask him to withdraw from this fight before it's too late." Swinging into the saddle, I added: "It's already too late for you. You love me and you know it. Tell Morgan Park that, and tell him I'm coming back to break him with my hands."

V

Riding into Hattan's Point, I was a man well known. Rollie Pinder was dead, and they knew whose gun had downed him. Maclaren's riders had been held off and made a laughingstock, and I had taken up Ball's fight to hold his ranch. Some men hated me for this, some admired me, and many thought me a fool.

All I knew was the horse between my knees, the guns on my thighs, and the blood of me pounding. My buckskin lifted his head high and moved down the dusty street like a dancer, for riding into this town was a challenge to them all. They knew it and I knew it. Leaving my horse behind Mother O'Hara's, I walked to the saloon and went in.

By then I'd taken time to shave, and, although

the pallor of sickness was on my face, there was none in my eyes or heart. It did me good to see their eyes widen and to hear my spurs jingle as I walked to the bar.

"Rye," I said, "the best you've got."

Key Chapin was there and, sitting with him, Morgan Park. The big man's eyes were cold as they stared at me. "I'm buying, gentlemen," I said, "and that includes you, Morgan Park, although you slug a man when his hands are down."

Park blinked. It had been a long time since anyone had told him off to his face. "And you, Key Chapin. It has always been my inclination to encourage freedom of the press and to keep my public relations on a good basis. And today I might even offer you a news item, something to read like this . . . Matt Sabre, of the Two Bar, was in town Friday afternoon. Matt is recovering from a bullet wound incurred during a minor dispute with Rollie Pinder, but is returning to the Two Bar to take up where he left off."

Chapin smiled. "That will be news to Jim Pinder. He didn't expect you back."

"He should have," I assured him. "I'm back to punish every murdering skunk who killed old man Ball."

All eyes were on me now, and Park was staring, not knowing what to make of me.

"Do you know who they are?" Chapin asked curiously.

"Definitely!" I snapped the word. "Every man of them . . ." I shifted my eyes to Park—"is known . . . with one exception. When Ball was dying, he named a man to me. Only I am not sure."

"Who?" demanded Chapin.

"Morgan Park," I said.

The big man came to his feet with a lunge. His brown face was ugly with hatred. "That's a lie!" he roared.

My shoulders lifted. "Probably a misunderstanding. I'll not take offense at your language, Mister Park, because it is a dead man you are calling a liar, and not I. Ball might have meant that one of your riders, a man named Lyell, was there. He died before he could be questioned. If it is true, I'll kill you after I whip you."

"Whip me?" Park's bellow was amazed. "Whip me? Why, you . . ."

"Unfortunately, I'm not sufficiently recovered from my wounds to do it today, but don't be impatient. You'll get your belly full of it when the time comes." Turning my back on him, I lifted my glass. "Gentlemen, your health!" And then I walked out of the place.

There was the good rich smell of cooked food and coffee when I opened the door of Mother O'Hara's. "Ah? It's you, then. And still alive. Things ain't what they used to be around here. Warned off by Maclaren, threatened by Jim

Pinder, beaten by Morgan Park, and you're still here."

"Still here an' staying, Katie O'Hara," I said, grinning at her, "and I've just said that and more to Morgan Park."

"There's been men die, and you've had the killin' of some."

"That's the truth, Katie, and I'd rather it never happened, but it's a hard country and small chance for a man who hesitates to shoot when the time comes. All the same, it's a good country, this. A country where I plan to stay and grow my children, Katie. I'll go back to the Two Bar and build my home there."

"You think they'll let you? You think you can keep it?"

"They'll have no choice."

Behind me a door closed and the voice of Rud Maclaren was saying: "We'll have a choice. Get out of the country while you're alive!"

The arrogance in his voice angered me, so I turned and faced him. Canaval and Morgan Park had come with him. "The Two Bar is my ranch," I said, "and I'll be staying there. Do you think yourself a king that you can dictate terms to a citizen of a free country? You've let a small power swell your head, Maclaren. You think you have power when all you have is money. If you weren't the father of the girl I'm to marry, Maclaren, I'd break you just to show you this

140

is a free country and we want no barons here."

His face mottled and grew hard. "Marry my daughter? You? I'll see you in hell first!"

"If you see me in hell, Maclaren," I said lightly, "you'll be seeing a married man, because I'm marrying Olga, and you can like it or light a shuck. I expect you were a good man once, but there's some that cannot stand the taste of power, and you're one." My eyes shifted to Morgan Park. "And there's another beside you. He has let his beef get him by too long. He uses force where you use money, but his time is running out, too. He couldn't break me when he had the chance, and, when my times comes, I'll break him."

More than one face in the room was approving, even if they glared at me, these two. "The trouble is obvious," I continued. "You've never covered enough country. You think you're sitting in the center of the world whereas you're just a couple of two-bit operators in a forgotten corner."

Turning my back on them, I helped myself to the Irish stew. Maclaren went out, but Park came around the table and sat down, and he was smiling. The urge climbed up in me to beat the big face off him and down him in the dirt as he had me. He was wider than me by inches, and taller. The size of his wrists and hands was amazing, yet he was not all beef, for he had brains and there was trouble in him, trouble for me. He was there to eat and said nothing to me.

• • •

When I returned to my horse, there was a man
sitting there. He looked up and I was astonished
at him. His face was like an unhappy monkey and
he was without a hair to the top of his head. Near
as broad in the shoulders as Morgan Park, he was
shorter than me by inches. "By the look of you,"
he said, "you'll be Matt Sabre."

"You're right, man. What is it about?"

"Katie O'Hara was a-tellin' me it was a man
you needed at the Two Bar. Now I'm a handy
all-around man, Mister Sabre, a rough sort of
gunsmith, hostler, blacksmith, carpenter, good
with an axe. An' I shoot a bit, know Cornish-style
wrestlin', an' am afraid of no man when I've my
two hands before me. I'm not so handy with a
short gun, but I've a couple of guns of my own
that I handle nice."

He got to his feet, and he could have been
nothing over five feet four but weighed all of two
hundred pounds, and his shirt at the neck showed
a massive chest covered with black hair and a
neck like a column of oak.

"The fact that you've the small end of a fight
appeals to me." He jerked his head toward the
door. "Katie has said I'm to go to work for you
an' she'd not take it kindly if I did not."

"You're Katie's man, then?"

His eyes twinkled amazingly. "Katie's man?
I'm afraid there's no such. She's a broth of a

woman, that one." He grinned up at me. "Is it a job I have?"

"When I've the ranch back," I agreed, "you've a job."

"Then let's be gettin' it back. Will you wait for me? I've a mule to get."

The mule was a dun with a face that showed all the wisdom, meanness, and contrariness that have been the traits of the mule since time began. With a tow sack behind the saddle and another before him, we started out of town. "My name is Brian Mulvaney," he said. "Call me what you like."

He grinned widely when he saw me staring at the butts of the two guns that projected from his boot tops. "These," he said, "are the Neal Bootleg pistol, altered by me to suit my taste. The caliber is Thirty-Five, but good. Now this"—from his waistband he drew a gun that lacked only wheels to make an admirable artillery piece—"this was a Mills Seventy-Five caliber. Took me two months of work off and on, but I've converted her to a four-shot revolver. A fine gun," he added.

All of seventeen inches long, it looked fit to break a man's wrists, but Mulvaney had powerful hands and arms. No man ever hit by a chunk of lead from that gun would need a doctor.

Four horses were in the corral at the Two Bar, and the men were strongly situated behind a log barricade. Mulvaney grinned at me. "What'd you suppose I've in this sack, laddie?" he demanded, his eyes twinkling. "I, who was a miner, also?"

"Powder?"

"Exactly! In those new-fangled sticks. Now, unless it makes your head ache too much, help me cut a few o' these sticks in half."

When that was done, he cut the fuses very short and slid caps into the sticks of powder. "Come now, me boy, an' we'll slip down close under the cover o' darkness, an' you'll see them takin' off like you never dreamed."

Crawling as close as we dared, each of us lit a fuse and hurled a stick of powder. My own stick must have landed closer to them than I planned, for we heard a startled exclamation followed by a yell. Then a terrific explosion blasted the night apart. Mulvaney's followed, and then we hastily hurled a third and a fourth.

One man lunged over the barricade and started straight for us. The others had charged the corral. The man headed our way suddenly saw us, and, wheeling, he fled as if the devil was after him. Four riders gripping only mane holds dashed from the corral, and then there was silence.

Mulvaney got to his feet, chuckling. "For guns they'd have stood until hell froze over, but the powder, the flyin' rocks, an' dust scared 'em good. An' you've your ranch back."

We had eaten our midday meal the next day, when I saw a rider approaching. It was Olga Maclaren.

"Nice to see you," I said, aware of the sudden tension her presence always inspired.

She was looking toward the foundation we had laid for the new house. It was on a hill with the long sweep of Cottonwood Wash before it. "You should be more careful," she said. "You had a visitor last night."

"We just took over last night," I objected. "Who do you mean?"

"Morgan. He was out here shortly after our boys got home. He met the bunch you stampeded from here."

"He's been puzzling me," I admitted. "Who is he? Did he come from around here?"

"I don't know. He's not talkative, but I've heard him mention places back East. I know he's been in Philadelphia and New York, but nothing else about him except that he goes to Salt Lake and San Francisco occasionally."

"Not back East?"

"Never since we've known him."

"You like him?"

She looked up at me. "Yes, Morgan can be very wonderful. He knows a lot about women and the things that please them." There was a flicker of laughter in her eyes. "He probably

145

doesn't know as much about them as you."

"Me?" I was astonished. "What gave you that idea?"

"Your approach that first day. You knew it would excite my curiosity, and a man less sure of himself would never have dared. If you knew no more about women than most Western men, you would have hung back, wishing you could meet me, or you would have got drunk to work up your courage."

"I meant what I said that day. You're going to marry me."

"Don't say that. Don't even think it. You've no idea what you are saying or what it would mean."

"Because of your father?" I looked at her. "Or Morgan Park?"

"You take him too lightly, Matt. I think he is utterly without scruple. I believe he would stop at nothing."

There was more to come and I was interested.

"There was a young man here from the East," she continued, "and I liked him. Knowing Morgan, I never mentioned him in Morgan's presence. Then one day he asked me about him. He added that it would be better for all concerned if the man did not come around anymore. Inadvertently I mentioned the young man's name, Arnold D'Arcy. When he heard that name, he became very disturbed. Who was he? Why had he come here? Had he asked any questions about anybody? Or described anybody he might be looking for? He asked me all those questions, but at the same time I thought little about it. Afterward, I began to believe that he was not merely jealous. Right then I decided to tell Arnold about it when he returned."

"And did you?"

There was a shadow of worry on her face. "No. He never came again." She looked quickly at me. "I've often thought of it. Morgan never mentioned him again, but somehow Arnold hadn't seemed like a man who would frighten easily."

Later, when she was mounting to leave, I asked her: "Where was D'Arcy from? Do you remember?"

"Virginia, I believe. He had served in the Army, and before coming West had been working in Washington."

Watching her go, I thought again of Morgan Park. He might have frightened D'Arcy away, but I could not shake off the idea that something vastly more sinister lay behind it. And Park had been close to us during the night. If he had wanted to kill me, it could have been done, but apparently he wanted me alive. Why?

"Mulvaney," I suggested, "if you can hold this place, I'll ride to Silver Reef and get off a couple of messages."

147

He stretched his huge arms and grinned at me. "Do you doubt it? I'll handle it or them. Go, and have yourself a time."

And in the morning, I was in the saddle again.

VI

High noon, and a mountain shaped like flame. Beyond the mountain and around it was a wide land with no horizons, but only the shimmering heat waves that softened all lines to vagueness and left the desert an enchanted land without beginning and without end.

As I rode, my mind studied the problem created by the situation around Cottonwood Wash. There were at least three, and possibly four sides to the question. Rud Maclaren with his Bar M, Jim Pinder with his CP, and myself with the Two Bar. The fourth possibility was Morgan Park.

Olga's account of Arnold D'Arcy's disappearance had struck a chord of memory. During ten years of my life I had been fighting in foreign wars, and there had been a military observer named D'Arcy, a Major Leo D'Arcy, who had been in China during the fighting there. It stuck in my mind that he had a brother named Arnold.

It was a remote chance, yet a possibility. Why did the name upset Park? What had become of Arnold? Where did Park come from? Pinder could be faced with violence and handled with violence. Maclaren might be circumvented. Morgan Park worried me.

Silver Reef lay sprawled in haphazard comfort along a main street and a few cross streets. There were the usual frontier saloons, stores, churches, and homes. The sign on the Elk Horn Saloon caught my attention. Crossing to it, I pushed through the door into the dim interior. While the bartender served me, I glanced around, liking the feel of the place.

"Rye?" The smooth-pated bartender squinted at me.

"Uhn-huh. How's things in the mines?"

"So-so. But you ain't no miner." He glanced at my cowhand's garb and then at the guns in their tied-down holsters. "This here's a quiet town. We don't see many gun handlers around here. The place for them is over east of here."

"Hattan's Point?"

"Yeah. I hear the Bar M an' CP both are hirin' hands. Couple of *hombres* from there rode into town a few days ago. One of 'em was the biggest man I ever did see."

Morgan Park in Silver Reef! That sounded interesting, but I kept a tight rein on my thoughts and voice. "Did he say anything about what was goin' on over there?"

"Not to me. The feller with him, though, he was inquirin' around for the Slade boys, Sam and

149

Jack. Gunslicks, both of them. The big feller, he never come in here a-tall. I seen him on the street a couple of times, but he went to the Wells Fargo Bank and down the street to see that shyster, Jake Booker."

"You don't seem to like Booker."

"Him? He's plumb no good! The man's a crook!"

Once started on Booker, the bartender told me a lot. Morgan Park had been in town before, but never came to the Elk Horn. He confined his visits to the back room of a dive called the Sump or occasional visits to the office of Jake Booker. The only man whoever came with him was Lyell.

Leaving the saloon, I sent off my telegram to Leo D'Arcy. Then I located the office of Booker, spotted the Sump, and considered the situation. Night came swiftly and miners crowded the street, a good-natured shoving, pushing, laughing throng, jamming the saloons and drinking. The crowd relaxed me with its rough good humor, and for the night I fell into it, drifting, joking, listening.

Turning off the street near Louder's store, I passed the street lamp on the corner, and for an instant was outlined in its radiance. From the shadows, flame stabbed. There was a tug at my sleeve, and then my own gun roared, and, as the shot sped, I went after it.

A man lunged from the side of the store and

ran staggeringly toward the alley behind it. Pistol ready, I ran after him. He wheeled, slipped, and was running again. He brought up with a crash against the corral bars, and fell. He was crawling to his feet, and I caught a glimpse of his face in the glow from the window. It was Lyell.

One hand at his throat, I jerked him erect. His face was gaunt and there was blood on his shirt front. He had been hit hard by my sudden, hardly aimed shot. "Got you, didn't I?"

"Yes, damn you, an' I missed. Put . . . put me down."

Lowering him to the ground, I dropped to one knee. "I'll get a doctor. I saw a sign up the street."

He grabbed my sleeve. "Ain't no use. I feel it. You got me good. Anyway"—he stared at me—"why should you get a doc for me?"

"I shouldn't. You were in the gang killed Ball."

His eyes bulged. "No! No, I wasn't there! He was a good old man! I wasn't in that crowd."

"Was Morgan Park there?"

His eyes changed, veiled. "Why would he be there? That wasn't his play."

"What's he seeing Booker for? What about Sam Slade?"

Footsteps crunched on the gravel, and a man carrying a lantern came up the alley.

"Get a doctor, will you? This man's been shot."

The man started off at a run and Lyell lay quietly, a tough, unshaven man with brown eyes.

He breathed hoarsely for several minutes while I uncovered the wound. "The Slades are to get Canaval. Park wants you for himself."

"What does he want? Range?"

"No. He . . . he wants money."

The doctor hurried up with the lantern carrier. Watching him start work, I backed away and disappeared in the darkness. If anybody knew anything about Park's plans, it would be Booker, and I had an idea I could get into Booker's office.

Booker's office was on the second floor of a frame building reached by an outside stairway. Once up there, a man would be fairly trapped if anyone came up those stairs. Down the street a music box was jangling, and the town showed no signs of going to sleep. Studying that stairway, I liked no part of it. Booker had many friends here, but I had none, and going up there would be a risk. Then I remembered all the other times I'd had no friends, so I hitched my guns easier on my thighs and went across the street.

Going up the steps two at a time, I paused at the door. Locks were no problem to a man of my experience and a minute later I was inside a dark office, musty with stale tobacco. Swiftly I checked the tray on the desk, the top drawer, and then the side drawers, lighting my exploration with a stump of candle. Every sense alert, ears attuned to the slightest sound, I worked rapidly, suddenly coming to an assayer's report. No location was mentioned, no notation on the sheet, but the ore had been rich, amazingly rich. Then among some older papers at the bottom of a drawer I found a fragment of a letter from Morgan Park, signed with his name.

You have been recommended to me as a man of discretion who could turn over a piece of property for a quick profit and who could handle negotiations with a buyer. I am writing for an appointment and will be in Silver Reef on the 12th. It is essential that this business remain absolutely confidential.

It was little enough, but a hint. I left the assayer's report but pocketed the letter. The long ride had tired me, for my wounds, while much improved, had robbed me of strength. Dousing the candle, I returned it to its shelf. And then I heard a low mutter of voices and steps on the stair.

Backing swiftly, I glanced around and saw a closed door that must lead to an inner room. Stepping through it, I closed it just in time. It was a room used for storage. Voices sounded and a door closed. A match scratched, and light showed under the door.

"Nonsense! Probably got in some drunken brawl! You're too suspicious, Morgan."

"Maybe, but the man worries me. He rides too

much, and he may get to nosing around and find something."

"Did you see Lyell before he died?"

"No. He shot first, though. Some fool saw him take a bead on somebody. This other fellow followed it up and killed him."

The crabbed voice of Booker interrupted. "Forget him. Forget Sabre. My men are lined up and they have the cold cash ready to put on the line! We haven't any time for child's play! I've done my part and now it's up to you! Get Sabre out of the way and get rid of Maclaren!"

"That's not so easy," Park objected stubbornly. "Maclaren is never alone, and, if anybody ever shot at him, he'd turn the country upside down to find the man. And after he is killed, the minute we step in, suspicion will be diverted to us."

"Nonsense!" Booker replied irritably. "Nobody knows we've had dealings. They'll have to settle the estate and I'll step in as representative of the buyers. Of course, if you were married to the girl, it would simplify things. What's the matter? Sabre cutting in there, too?"

"Shut up!" Park's voice was ugly. "If you ever say a thing like that again, I'll wring you out like a dirty towel, Booker. I mean it."

"You do your part," Booker said, "and I'll do mine. The buyers have the money and they are ready. They won't wait forever."

A chair scraped and Park's heavy steps went

to the door and out. There was a faint squeak of a cork twisting in a bottle neck, the gargle of a poured drink, then the bottle and glass returned to the shelf. The light vanished and a door closed. Then footsteps grated on the gravel below. Only a minute behind him, I hurried from the vicinity, then paused, sweating despite the cool air. Thinking of what I'd heard, I retrieved my horse and slipped quietly out of town. Bedded down among the clustering cedars, I thought of that, and then of Olga, the daughter of Maclaren, of her soft lips, the warmth of her arms, the quick proud lift of her chin.

Coming home to Cottonwood Wash and the Two Bar with the wind whispering through the greasewood and rustling the cottonwood leaves, I kept a careful watch but saw nobody until Mulvaney himself stepped into sight.

"Had any trouble?" I asked him.

"Trouble? None here," he replied. "Some men came by, but the sound of my Spencer drove them away again." He walked to the door. "There's grub on the table. How was it in Silver Reef?"

"A man killed."

"Be careful, lad. There's too many dyin'."

When I had explained, he nodded. "Do they know it was you?"

"I doubt it." It felt good to be back on my own place again, seeing the white-faced cattle browsing in the pasture below, seeing the water flowing to irrigate the small garden we'd started.

"You're tired." Mulvaney studied me. "But you look fit. You've thrown a challenge in the teeth of Park. You'll be backing it up?"

"Backing it up?" My eyes must have told what was in me. "That's one man I want, Mulvaney. He had me down and beat me, and I'll not live free until I whip him or he whips me fair."

"He's a power of man, lad. I've seen him lift a barrel of whiskey at arm's length overhead. It will be a job to whip him."

"Ever box any, Mulvaney? You told me you'd wrestled Cornish style."

"What Irishman hasn't boxed a bit? Is it a sparrin' mate you're wantin'? Sure 'n' it would be good to get the leather on my maulies again."

For a week we were at it, every night we boxed, lightly at first, then faster. He was a brawny man, a fierce slugger, and a powerful man in the clinches. On the seventh day, we did a full thirty minutes without a break. And in the succeeding days my strength returned and my speed grew greater. The rough-and-tumble part of it I loved. Nor was I worried about Morgan's knowing more tricks than I—the waterfronts are the place to learn the dirty side of fighting. I would use everything I'd learned there, if Morgan didn't fight fair.

It was after our tenth session with the gloves that Mulvaney stripped them off and shook his head admiringly. "Faith, lad, you've a power of muscle behind that wallop of yours. That last one came from nowhere and I felt it clean to my toes. Never did I believe a man lived that could hit like that."

"Thanks," I said. "I'm riding to town tomorrow."

"To fight him?"

"No, to see the girl, Olga Maclaren, to buy supplies, and perhaps to ride him a little. I want him furious before we fight. I want him mad . . . mad and wild."

He nodded wisely at me. "It'll help, for no man can fight unless he keeps his head. But be careful, lad. Remember they are gunnin' for you, an' there's nothin' that would better please them than to see you dead on the ground."

When the buckskin was watered, I returned him to the hitch rail and walked into the saloon. Hattan's Point knew that Lyell was dead, but they had no idea who had done it. Key Chapin was the first man I met, and I looked at him, wondering on which side he stood. He looked at me curiously and motioned toward the chair across the table from him. Dropping into it, I began to build a smoke.

"Well, Sabre, you're making quite a name for yourself."

I shrugged. "That's not important. All I want is a ranch."

"All?"

"And a girl."

"One may be as hard to get as the other."

"Maybe. Anyway, I've made a start on the ranch. In fact, I have the ranch and intend to keep it."

"Heard about Lyell?"

"Killed, wasn't he? Somewhere west of here?"

"At Silver Reef. It's a peaceful, quiet place in spite of being a boomtown. And they have a sheriff over there who believes in keeping it peaceful. They tell me he is working hard to find out who killed Lyell."

"It might be anybody. There was a rumor that he was one of the men in the raid on the Ball Ranch."

"And which you promised to bury on the spot."

What this was building to I did not know, but I was anxious to find out just where Chapin stood. He would be a good friend to have, and a bad enemy, for his paper had a good deal of influence around town.

"You told me when I first came here that the town was taking sides. Which is your side?"

He hesitated, toying with his glass. "That's a harder question to answer since you came," he replied frankly. "I will say this. I am opposed to violence. I believe now is the time to establish a peaceful community, and I believe it can be done. For that reason, I am opposed to the CP outfit whose code is violence."

"And Maclaren?"

He hesitated again. "Maclaren can be reasoned with at times. Stubborn, yes, but only because he has an exaggerated view of his own rightness. It is not easy to prove him wrong, but it can be done."

"And Park?"

He looked at me sharply, a cool, measuring glance as if to see what inspired the remark. Then he said: "Morgan Park is generally felt to see things as Maclaren does."

"Is that your opinion?"

He did not answer me, frowning as he stared out the door. Key Chapin was a handsome man, and an able one. I could understand how he felt about law and order. Basically, I agreed with him, but when I'm attacked, I can't take it lying down.

"Look, Chapin"—I leaned over the table— "I've known a dozen frontier towns tougher than this one. To each came law and order, but it took a fight to get them. The murderers, cheats, and swindlers must be stamped out before the honest citizens can have peace. And it's peace that I'm fighting for. You, more than anybody else, can build the situation to readiness for it with your paper. Write about it. Get the upright citizens prepared to enforce it, once this battle is over."

He nodded, then glanced at me. "What about you? You're a gunfighter. In such a community, there is no place for such a man."

That made me grin. "Chapin, I never drew a gun on a man in my life who didn't draw on me first, or try to. And while I may be a gunfighter, I'm soon to be a rancher and a solid citizen. Count on me to help."

"Even to stopping this war?"

"What war? Ball had a ranch. He was a peaceful old man who wanted no trouble from anyone, but he was weaker than the Bar M or the CP, so he died. He turned the ranch over to me on the condition that I keep it. If protecting one's property is war, then we'll have it for a long time."

"You could sell out."

"Run? Is that what you mean? I never ducked out of a good fight yet, Chapin, and never will. When they stop fighting me, I'll hang up my guns. Until then, I shall continue to fight." Filling my glass, I added: "Don't look at the overall picture so long that you miss the details."

"What do you mean?"

"Look for motives. What are the origins of this fight? I'd start investigating the participants, and I mean neither Maclaren nor Pinder." Getting up, I put my hat on my head, and added: "Ever hear of a man named Booker at Silver Reef? A lawyer?"

"He's an unmitigated scoundrel, and whatever

160

he does, he's apt to get away with. If there's a loophole in the law he doesn't know, then nobody knows it."

"Then find out why he's interested in this fight and, when the Slade boys drift into this country, ask yourself why they are here. Also, ask yourself why Morgan Park is meeting Booker in secret."

Olga was not in town, so I turned the buckskin toward the Bar M. A cowhand with one foot bandaged was seated on the doorstep when I rode up. He stared, his jaw dropping.

"Howdy," I said calmly, taking out the makings. "I'm visiting on the ranch and don't want any trouble. As far as you boys are concerned, I've no hard feelings."

"You've no hard feelin's! What about me? You durned near shot my foot off!"

I grinned at him. "Next time you'll stay under cover. Anyway, what are you griping about? You haven't done a lick of work since it happened!"

Somebody chuckled. I looked around and saw Canaval. "I reckon he did it on purpose, Sabre."

"Excuse me?" the injured man roared. Disgusted, he rose and limped off.

"What you want here, Sabre?" Canaval asked, still smiling.

"Just visiting."

"Sure you're welcome?"

"No, I'm not sure. But if you're wondering if I came looking for trouble, I didn't. If trouble comes to me on this ranch now, it will be because I'm pushed, and pushed hard. If you're the guardian angel of peace, just relax. I'm courtin'.'"

"Rud won't take kindly to that. He may have me order you off."

"All right, Canaval, if he does, and you tell me to go, I'll go. Only one thing . . . you keep Park off me. I'm not ready for him, and, when it comes, I'd rather she didn't see it."

"Fair enough." He tossed his cigarette into the yard. "You'll not be bothered under those circumstances. Only"—he grinned and his eyes twinkled—"you might be wrong about Olga. She might like to see you tangle with Park."

Starting up the steps, I remembered something. "Canaval!"

He turned sharply, ready on the instant.

"A friendly warning," I said. "Some of the people who don't like me also want your boss out of here. To get him out, you have to go first. If you hear of the Slades in this country, you'll know they've come for you and your boss."

His eyes searched mine. "The Slades?"

"Yeah, for you and Maclaren. Somebody is saving me for dessert."

He was standing there, looking after me, when I knocked.

Inside a voice answered that set my blood pounding. "Come in!"

VII

As I entered, there was an instant when my reflection was thrown upon the mirror beside hers. Seeing my gaze over her shoulder, she turned, and we stood there, looking at ourselves in the mirror—a tall, dark young man in a dark blue shirt, black silk neckerchief, black jeans, and tied-down holsters with their walnut-stocked guns, and Olga in a sea-green gown, filmy and summery-looking.

She turned quickly to face me. "What are you doing here? My father will be furious!"

"He'll have to get over it sometime, and it might as well be right now."

She searched my face. "You're still keeping up that foolish talk? About marrying me?"

"It isn't foolish. Have you started buying your trousseau?"

"Of course not!"

"You'd better. You'll need something to wear, and I won't have much money for a year or two."

"Matt"—her face became serious—"you'd better go. I'm expecting Morgan."

I took her hands. "Don't worry. I promised Canaval there would be no trouble, and there will be none, no matter what Morgan Park wants to do or tries to do."

She was unconvinced and tried to argue, but

I was thinking how lovely she was. Poised, her lovely throat bare, she was something to set a man's pulses pounding.

"Matt!" She was angry now. "You're not even listening! And don't look at me like that!"

"How else should a man look at a woman? And why don't we sit down? Is this the way you receive guests at the Bar M? At the Two Bar we are more thoughtful."

"So I've heard," she said dryly. Her anger faded. "Matt? How do you feel? I mean those wounds? Are they all right?"

"Not all right, but much better. I'm not ready for Morgan Park yet, but I will be soon. He won't be missed much when he's gone."

"Gone?" She was surprised. "Remember that I like Morgan."

"Not very much." I shrugged. "Yes, gone. This country isn't big enough to hold both of us even if you weren't in it."

She sat down opposite me and her face was flushed a little. She looked at me, then looked away, and neither of us said anything for a long minute.

"It's nice here," I said at last. "Your father loves this place, doesn't he?"

"Yes, only I wish he would be content and stop trying to make it bigger."

"Men like your father never seem to learn when they have enough."

"You don't talk like a cowhand, Matt."

"That's because I read a book once."

"Key told me you had been all over the world. He checked up on you. He said you had fought in China and South Africa."

"That was a long time ago."

"How did you happen to come West?"

"I was born in the West, and then I always wanted to return to it and have a ranch of my own, but there wasn't anything to hold me down, so I just kept on drifting from place to place. Staying in one place did not suit me unless there was a reason to stay, and there never was . . . before."

Tendrils of her dark hair curled against her neck. The day was warm, and I could see tiny beads of perspiration on her upper lip. She stood up suddenly, uneasily. "Matt, you'd better go. Father will be coming and he'll be furious."

"And Morgan Park will be coming. And it doesn't matter in the least whether they come or not. I came here to see you, and, as long as they stay out of the way, there'll be no trouble."

"But, Matt . . ." She stepped closer to me, and I took her by the elbows. She started to step back, but I drew her to me swiftly. I took her chin and turned her head slightly. She resisted, but the continued pressure forced her chin to come around. She looked at me then, her eyes wide and more beautiful than I would ever have believed eyes could be, and then I kissed her.

We stood there, clinging together tightly, and then she pulled violently away from me. For an instant she looked at me, and then she moved swiftly to kiss me again, and we were like that when hoofs sounded in the yard. Two horses.

We stepped apart, but her eyes were wide and her face was pale when they came through the door, her breast heaving and her white teeth clinging to her lower lip. They came through the door, Rud Maclaren first, and then Morgan Park, dwarfing Maclaren in spite of the fact that he was a big man. When they saw me, they stopped.

Park's face darkened with angry blood. He started toward me, his voice hoarse with fury. "Get out! Get out, I say!"

My eyes went past him to Maclaren. "Is Park running this place, or are you? It seems to me he's got a lot of nerve, ordering people off the place of Rud Maclaren."

Maclaren flushed. He didn't like my being there, but he disliked Park's usurping of authority even more. "That'll do, Morgan! I'll order people out of my own home!"

Morgan Park's face was ugly at that minute, but, before he could speak, Canaval appeared in the door. "Boss, Sabre said he was visitin', not huntin' trouble. He said he would make no trouble and would go when I asked him. He also said he would make no trouble with Park."

Before Maclaren could reply, Olga said quickly: "Father, Mister Sabre is my guest. When the time comes, he will leave. Until then, I wish him to stay."

"I won't have him in this house!" Maclaren said angrily. He strode to me, the veins in his throat swelling. "Damn you, Sabre! You've a gall to come here after shootin' my men, stealin' range that rightly belongs to me, an' runnin' my cattle out of Cottonwood Wash!"

"Perhaps," I admitted, "there's something in what you say, but I think we have no differences we can't settle without fighting. Your men came after me first. I never wanted trouble with you, Rud, and I think we can reach a peaceful solution."

It took the fire out of him. He was still truculent, still wanting to throw his weight around, but mollified. Right then I sensed the truth about Rud Maclaren. It was not land and property he wanted so much as to be known as the biggest man in the country. He merely knew of no way to get respect and admiration other than through wealth and power.

Realizing that gave me an opening. "I was talking to Chapin today. If we are going to be safe, we must stop all this fighting, and the only way it can be done is through the leadership of the right man. I think you're that man, Maclaren."

He was listening, and he liked what he heard.

167

"You're the big man of the community," I added. "If you make a move for peace, others will follow."

"The Pinders wouldn't listen," he protested. "You know that. You killed Rollie, but if you hadn't, Canaval might have. Jim will never rest until you're dead. And he hates me and all I stand for."

Morgan Park was listening, his eyes hard and watchful. He had never imagined that Maclaren and I would talk peace, and, if we reached a settlement, his plans were finished.

"If Pinder and the CP were alone, they would have to become outlaws to persist in this fight. If the fight continues, all the rustlers in the country will come in here to run off our herds while we fight. Did it ever fail? When honest men fall out, thieves always profit. Moreover, you'll break yourself paying gunman's wages. From now on they'll come higher."

Olga was listening with some surprise and, I believed, with respect. Certainly I had gone further than I had ever believed possible. My own instinct is toward fighting, yet I have always been aware of the futility of it. Now I could see that, if the fighting ended, all our problems would be simple and easily settled. The joker in the deck was Morgan Park; he had everything to lose by a settlement, and nothing to gain.

Park interrupted suddenly. "I wouldn't trust all

this talk, Rud. Sabre sounds good, but he's got some trick in mind. What's he planning? What's he trying to cover?"

"Morgan!" Olga protested. "I'm surprised at you. Matt is sincere and you know it."

"I know nothing of the kind," he replied shortly. "I'm surprised that you would defend this . . . this killer."

He was looking at me as he spoke, and it was then I said the one thing I had wanted to say, the hunch I could not prove. "At least," I replied, "my killings have been in fair fights, by men trying to kill me. I've never killed a man who had no gun, and who would have been helpless against me in any case."

Morgan Park stiffened and his face grew livid. Yet I knew from the way his eyes searched my face that he detected the undercurrent of meaning and he was trying to gauge the depth of my knowledge. It was D'Arcy I had in mind, for D'Arcy had known something about Park and had been slain for what he knew, or because he might tell others what he knew. I was sure of that.

"It isn't only rustlers," I continued to Maclaren, "but others have schemes they can only bring to success through trouble here. There are those who wish this fight to continue so they may get rights and claims they could never secure if there was peace."

Morgan Park was glaring, fighting for control.

He could see that unless he kept his temper and acted quickly his plans might be ruined. Something of what I'd said apparently touched Maclaren, for he was nodding.

"I'll have to think it over," Maclaren said. "This is no time to make decisions."

"By all means." Turning, I took Olga's arm. "Now if you'll excuse us?"

Morgan's face was a study in concentrated fury. He started forward, blood in his eye. Putting Olga hurriedly to one side, I was ready for him, but Canaval stepped between us.

"Hold it!" Canaval's command stopped Park in his tracks. "That's all, Park. We'll have no trouble here."

"What's the matter?" he sneered. "Sabre need a nursemaid now?"

"No." The foreman was stiff. "He gave me his word, and I gave mine. As long as he is on this place, my word holds. If the boss wants him to go, he'll go."

In the silence that followed, Maclaren turned to me. "Sabre, I've no reason to like you, but you are my daughter's guest and you talk straight from the shoulder. Remain as long as you like."

Park started to speak, but realized he could do nothing. He turned his heavy head, staring at me from under heavy brows. That gaze was cold and deadly. "We can settle our differences elsewhere, Sabre."

Olga was worried when we got outside. "You shouldn't have come, Matt. There'll be trouble. Morgan is a bad enemy."

"He was my enemy, anyway. That he is a bad enemy, I know. I think another friend of yours found that out."

She looked up quickly, real fear in her eyes. "What do you mean?"

"Your friend, D'Arcy. He comes of a family that does not frighten easily. Did you ever have a note of acknowledgement from him?"

"No."

"Strange. I'd have said such a man would never neglect such an obvious courtesy."

We stood together then, looking out at the night and the desert, no words between us but needing no words, our hearts beating together, our blood moving together, feeling the newness of love discovered. The cottonwood leaves brushed their pale green hands together, and their muted whispering seemed in tune with our own thoughts. This was my woman. The one I would walk down the years with. The leaves said that and my blood said it, and I knew the same thoughts were in her, reluctant as she might be to admit it.

"This trouble will pass," I said softly, taking her hand, "as the night will pass, and, when it has gone, and the winds have blown the dust away, then I shall take you to Cottonwood Wash . . . to live." Her hand stayed in mine, and I continued. "We'll build something there to last down the years until this will all seem a bad dream, a nightmare dissipated by the morning sunlight."

"But could you ever settle down? Could you stay?"

"Of course. Men don't wander for the love only of wandering. They wander because they are in search of something. A place of one's own, a girl, a job accomplished. It is only you who has mattered since the day I rode into the streets of Hattan's Point and saw you there."

Turning toward her, I took her by the elbows and, her breath caught, then came quickly and deeply, her lips parted slightly as she came into my arms, and I felt her warm body melt against mine, and her lips were warm and seeking, urgent, passionate. My fingers ran into her hair and along her scalp, and her kisses hurt my lips as mine must have hurt hers. All the fighting, all the waiting melted into nothingness then.

She pulled back suddenly, frightened yet excited, her breast rising and falling as she fought for control. "This isn't good! We're . . . we're too violent. We've got to be more calm."

I laughed then, full of the zest of living and loving and seeing the glory of her there in the moonlight. I laughed and took her arms again. "You're not exactly a calm person."

"I?" A flush darkened her face. "Well, all right then. Neither of us is calm."

"Need we be?" My hands reached for her, and then I heard someone whistling, and irritably I looked up to hear feet grating on the gravel path.

It was Canaval. "Better ride," he said. "I wouldn't put it past Park to dry-gulch a man."

"Canaval!" Olga protested. "How can you say that?"

His slow eyes turned to her. "You think so, too, ma'am. You always was an uncommon smart girl. You've known him for what he was for a mighty long time." He turned back to me. "Mean what you said back there? About peace and all?"

"You bet I did. What can we gain by fighting?"

"You're right," Canaval agreed, "but there'll be bloodshed before it's over. Pinder won't quit. He hates Rud Maclaren and now he hates you. He won't back up or quit." Canaval turned to Olga. "Let me talk to Sabre alone, will you? There's something he should know."

"All right." She gave me her hand. "Be careful. And good night."

We watched her walk back up the path, and, when my eyes turned back to him, his were surprisingly soft. I could see his expression even in the moonlight. "Reminds me of her mother," he said quietly.

"You knew her?" I was surprised.

"She was my sister."

That was something I could never have guessed.

"She doesn't know," he explained. "Rud and I used to ride together. I was too fast with a gun and killed a man with too many relatives. I left and Rud married my sister. From time to time we wrote, and, when Rud was having trouble with rustlers, I came out to lend a hand. He persuaded me to stay."

He looked around at me. "One thing more. What did you mean about the Slades?"

So I told him in detail of my trip to Silver Reef, the killing of Lyell, and the conversation I'd overheard between Park and Booker. Where I had heard the conversation, I did not tell him, and only said there was some deal between the two of them that depended upon results to be obtained by Morgan Park.

It was after midnight when I finally left the Bar M, turning off the main trail and cutting across country for the head of Gypsum Cañon.

Mulvaney was waiting for me. "Knowed the horse's walk," he explained. Nodding toward the hills, he added: "Too quiet out there."

The night was clear, wide, and peaceful. Later, during the night, I awakened with a start, the sound of a shot ringing in my ears. Mulvaney

174

was sleeping soundly, so I did not disturb him. Afterward, all was quiet, so I dropped off to sleep once more.

In the morning I mentioned it to Mulvaney.

"Did you get up?" he asked.

"Yeah. Went out in the yard and listened, but heard nothing more. Could have been a hunter. Maybe one of the Benaras boys."

Two hours later I knew better. Riding past Maverick Spring, I saw the riderless horse grazing near a dark bundle that lay on the grass. The dark bundle was Rud Maclaren, and he was dead. He had been shot twice from behind, both shots through the head. He was sprawled on his face, both hands above his head, one knee drawn up. Both guns were in their holsters, and his gun belt was tied down. After one look, I stood back and fired three shots as a signal to Mulvaney.

When he saw Maclaren, his face went white and he looked up. "You shouldn't have done it, boy. The country hated him but they respected him, too. They'll hang a man for this!"

"Don't be foolish!" I was irritated but appalled, too. "I didn't do this! Feel of him! It must have been that shot I heard last night."

"He's cold, all right. This'll blow the lid off, Matt. You'd best rig a story for them. And it had better be good!"

"No rigging. I'll tell the truth."

"They'll hang you, Matt. They'll never believe

you didn't do it." He waved a hand around. "He's on your place. The two of you have been feudin'. They'll say you shot him in the back."

Standing over the body with the words of Mulvaney in my ears, I could see with piercing clarity the situation I was in. What could he have been doing here? Why would he come to my ranch in the middle of the night?

I could see their accusing eyes when the death was reported, the shock to Olga, the reaction of the people, the accusations of Park. Somebody wanted Maclaren dead enough to shoot him in the back. Who?

VIII

Strangely the morning was cool with a hint of rain. Mulvaney, at my request, had gone to the Bar M to tell Canaval of the killing, and it was up to Canaval to tell Olga. I did not like to think of that. My luck held in one sense, for Jolly Benaras came riding up the wash, and I asked him to ride to Hattan's Point to report to Key Chapin.

Covering the body with a tarp, I mounted and began to scout the area. How much time I had, I did not know, but it could not be much. Soon they would be arriving from Hattan's Point, and even sooner from the Bar M. One thing puzzled me. There had been but one shot fired, but there were two bullet holes in Maclaren's skull.

Carefully I examined the sand under the body and was struck by a curious thing. There was no blood! None on the sand, that is. There was plenty of blood on Rud himself, but all of it, strangely enough, seemed to come from one bullet hole. There was a confusion of tracks where his horse had moved about while he lay there on the ground, but at this point the wash was sandy, and no definite track could be distinguished. Then horses' hoofs sounded, and I looked up to see five riders coming toward me. The nearest was Canaval, and, beside him, Olga. The others were all Bar M riders, and from one glance at their faces I knew there was no doubt in their minds and little reason for speculation that I had killed Rud Maclaren.

Canaval drew up, and his eyes pierced mine, cold, calculating, and shrewd. Olga threw herself from her horse and ran to the still form on the ground. She had refused to meet my eyes or to notice me.

"This looks bad, Canaval. When did he leave the ranch?"

He studied me carefully, as if he were seeing me for the first time. "I don't know exactly," he said. "No one heard him go. He must have pulled out sometime after two this morning."

"The shot I heard was close to four."

"One shot?"

"Only one . . . but he's been shot twice." Hesitating a little, I asked: "Who was with him when you last saw him?"

"He was alone. If it's Morgan Park you are thinkin' of, forget it. He left right after you did. When I last saw Rud, he was goin' to his room, feelin' mighty sleepy."

The Bar M riders were circling around. Their faces were cold and they started an icy chill coming up my spine. These men were utterly loyal, utterly ruthless when aroused. The night before they had given me the benefit of the doubt, but now they saw no reason to think of any other solution but the obvious one.

Tom Fox, a lean, hard-bitten Bar M man, was staring at me. Coolly he took a rope from his pommel. "What we waitin' for, men?" he asked bitterly. "There's our man."

Turning, I said: "Fox, from what I hear you're a good man and a good hand. Don't jump to any hasty conclusions. I didn't kill Rud Maclaren and had no reason to. We made peace talk last night and parted in good spirits."

Fox looked up at Canaval. "That right?"

Canaval hesitated, his expression unchanging. Then he spoke clearly. "It is . . . but Rud Maclaren changed his mind afterward."

"Changed his mind?" That I couldn't believe, yet at the expression in Canaval's eyes, I knew he was speaking the truth. "Even so," I added, "how could I be expected to know that? When I left, all was friendly."

"You couldn't know it," Canaval agreed, "unless he got out of bed an' came to tell you. He might have done that, and I can think of no other reason for him to come here. He came to tell you . . . an' you killed him when he started away."

The hands growled and Fox shook out a loop. It was Olga who stopped them. "No! Wait until the others arrive. If he killed my father, I want him to die! But wait until the others come."

Reluctantly Fox drew in his rope and coiled it. Sweat broke out on my forehead. I could fight, and I would if it came to that, but these men only believed they were doing the right thing. They had no idea that I was innocent. My mouth was dry and my hands felt cold. I tried to catch Olga's eye but she ignored me. Canaval seemed to be studying something, but he did not speak a word.

The first one to arrive was Key Chapin, and behind him a dozen other men. He looked at me, a quick, worried glance, and then looked at Canaval. Without waiting for questions, the foreman quietly repeated what had happened, telling of the entire evening, facts that could not until then have been known to the men.

"There's one thing," I said suddenly, "that I want to call to your attention."

They looked at me, but there was not a friendly eye in the lot of them. Looking around the circle

179

of their faces, I felt a cold sinking in my stomach, and a feeling came over me. *Matt Sabre,* I was telling myself, *this is the end. You've come to it at last, and you'll hang for another man's crime.*

Not one friendly face—and Mulvaney had not returned with the Bar M riders. There was no sign of Jolly Benaras.

"Chapin," I asked, "will you turn Maclaren over?"

The request puzzled them, and they looked from me to the covered body, then to Chapin. He swung down and walked across to the dead man. I heard Olga's breath catch, and then Chapin rolled Maclaren on his back.

He straightened up then, still puzzled. The others looked blankly at me.

"The reason you are so quick to accuse me is that he is here, on my ranch. Well, he was not killed here. There's no blood on the ground."

Startled, they all looked. Before any comment could be made, I continued: "One of the wounds bled badly, and the front of his shirt is dark with blood. The sand would be, too, if he'd been killed here. What I am saying is that he was killed elsewhere, then carried here!"

"But why?" Chapin protested.

Canaval said: "You mean to throw guilt onto you?"

"I sure do mean that. Also, that shot I heard fired was shot into him after he was dead."

Fox shook his head, and sneered: "How could you figure that?"

"A dead man does not bleed. Look at him. All the blood came from one wound."

Suddenly we heard more horsemen, and Mulvaney returned with his guns and the Benaras boys. Not one, but all of them.

Coolly they moved up to the edge of the circle.

"We'd be beholden," the elder Benaras said loudly, "if you'd all move back. We're friends to Sabre, an' we don't believe he done it. Now give him air an' listen."

They hesitated, not liking it. But their common sense told them that, if trouble started now, it would be a bloody mess. Carefully the nearest riders eased back. Whether Olga was listening, I had no idea. Yet it was she who I wanted most to convince.

"There are other men with axes to grind beside the Pinders and I," I said. "What had I to fear from Rud? Already I had shown I could take care of myself against all of them. Face to face, I was twice the man Rud was."

"You talk yourself up mighty well," Fox said.

"You had your chance in the cañon," I said brutally, "and, when I say I can hold this ranch, you know I'm not lying."

Horses came up the trail and the first faces I recognized were Bodie Miller and the redhead I'd whipped at the Two Bar. Bodie pushed his horse into the circle when he saw me. The devil was riding Bodie again, and I could see from Canaval's face that he knew it.

Right at the moment Bodie was remembering how I had dared him to gamble at point-blank range. "You, is it?" he said. "I'll kill you one day."

"Keep out of this, Bodie!" Canaval ordered sharply.

Miller's dislike was naked in his eyes. "Rud's dead now," he said. "Mebbe you won't be the boss anymore. Mebbe she'll want a younger man for boss!"

The import of his words was like a blow across the face. Suddenly I wanted to kill him, suddenly I was going to. Canaval's voice was a cool breath of air through my fevered brain. "That will be for Miss Olga to decide." He turned to her. "Do you wish me to continue as foreman?"

"Naturally." Her voice was cold and even, and in that moment I was proud of her. "And your first job will be to fire Bodie Miller!"

Miller's face went white with fury, and his lips bared back from his teeth. Before he could speak, I interfered. "Don't say it, Bodie! Don't say it!" I stepped forward to face him across Maclaren's body.

The malignancy of his expression was unbelievable. "You an' me are goin' to meet," he said, staring at me.

"When you're ready, Bodie." Deliberately, not wanting the fight here, now, I turned my back on him.

Chapin and Canaval joined me while the men loaded the body into a buckboard. "We don't think you're guilty, Sabre. Have you any ideas?"

"Only that I believe he was killed elsewhere and carried here to cast blame on me. I don't believe it was Pinder. He would never shoot Maclaren in the back."

"You think Park did it?" Canaval demanded.

"Peace between myself and Maclaren would be the last thing he'd want," I said.

Bob Benaras was waiting for me. "You can use Jonathan an' Jolly," he said. "I ain't got work enough to keep 'em out of mischief."

He was not fooling me in the least. "Thanks. I can use them to spell Mulvaney on look-out, and there's plenty of work to do."

For two weeks we worked hard, and the inquest of Rud Maclaren turned up nothing new. There had been no will, so the ranch went to Olga. Yet nothing was settled. Some people believed I had killed Maclaren, most of them did not know, but the country was quiet.

Of Bodie Miller we heard much. He killed a man at Hattan's Point in a saloon quarrel, shot him before he could get his hand on a gun. Bodie and his riding partner, Red, were riding with a lot of riff-raff from Hite. The Bar M was missing cattle and Bodie laughed when he heard it. He pistol-whipped a man in Silver Reef, and wounded a man while driving off the posse that came after him.

I worried more about Morgan Park. I had to discover just what his plan was. My only chance was to follow Park every hour of the day and night. I must know where he went, what he was doing, with whom he was talking. One night I waited on a hill above Hattan's Point, watching the house where he lived when in town.

When he came out of the house, I could feel the hackles rising on the back of my neck. There was something about him that would always stir me to fury, and it did now. Stifling it, I watched him go to Mother O'Hara's, watched him mount up, and ride out of town on the Bar M road. Yet scarcely a dozen miles from town he drew up and scanned his back trail. Safely outside of view, I watched him. Apparently satisfied with what he did not see, he turned right along the ridge, keeping under cover. He now took a course that led him into the wildest and most remote corner of the Bar M, that neck of land north of my own and extending far west. His trail led him out upon Dark Cañon Plateau. Knowing little of this area, I closed the distance between us until I saw him making camp.

Before daylight he was moving again. The

sun rose and the day became hot, with a film of heat haze obscuring all the horizons. He seemed headed toward the northwest where the long line of the Sweet Alice Hills ended the visible world. This country was a maze of cañons. To the south it fell away in an almost sheer precipice for hundreds of feet to the bottom of Dark Cañon. There were trails off the plateau, but I knew none of them.

The view was breathtaking, overlooking miles of columned and whorled sandstone, towering escarpments, minarets, and upended ledges. This had once been inhabited country for there were ruins of cliff dwellings about, and Indian writings.

The trail divided at the east end of the plateau and the flat rock gave no indication of which Park had taken. It looked as though I had lost him. Taking a chance, I went down a steep slide into Poison Cañon and worked back in the direction he must have taken, but the only tracks were of rodents and one of a bighorn sheep. Hearing a sound of singing, I dismounted. Rifle in hand, I worked my way through the rocks and brush.

"No use to shave," the man at the fire said. "We're stuck here. No chance to get to Hattan's Point now."

"Yeah?" The shaver scoffed. "You see that big feller? Him an' Slade are talking medicine. We'll move out soon. I don't want to get caught with no beard when I go to town."

"Who'll care how you look? An' maybe the fewer who know how you look, the better."

"After this show busts open," the shaver replied, "it ain't goin' to matter who knows me. We'll have that town sewed up tighter'n a drum."

"Mebbe." The cook straightened and rubbed his back. "Again, mebbe not. I wish it was rustlin' cows. Takin' towns can be mighty mean."

"It ain't the town, just a couple o' ranches. Only three, four men on the Two Bar, an' about the same on the Bar M. Slade will have the toughest job done afore we start."

"That big feller looks man enough to do it by himself. But if he can pay, his money will look good to me."

"He better watch his step. That Sabre ain't no chicken with a pair o' Colts. He downed Rollie Pinder, an' I figure it was him done for Lyell over to the Reef."

"It'll be somethin' when he an' Bodie git together. Both faster'n greased lightnin'."

"Sabre won't be around. Pinder figures on raidin' that spread today. Sam wouldn't help him because he'd promised Park. Pinder'll hit 'em about sundown, an' that'll be the end of Sabre."

Waiting no longer, I hurried back to my horse. If Pinder was to attack the Two Bar, Park would have to wait. Glancing at the sun, fear rose in my throat. It would be nip and tuck if I was to get back. Another idea came to me. I would rely on Mulvaney and the Benaras boys to protect the Two Bar. I would counterattack and hit the CP!

When I reached the CP, it lay deserted and still but for the cook, bald-headed and big-bellied. He rushed from the door but I was on him too fast, and he dropped his rifle under the threat of my six-gun. Tying him up, I dropped him in a feed bin and went to the house. Finding a can of wagon grease, I smeared it thickly over the floor in front of both doors and more of it on the steps. Leaving the door partly open, I dumped red pepper into a pan and balanced it above the door where the slightest push would send it cascading over whoever entered, filling the air with fine grains.

Opening the corral, I turned the horses loose and started them down the valley. Digging out all the coffee on the place, I packed it to take away, knowing how a cowhand dearly loves his coffee. It was my idea to make their lives as miserable as possible to get them thoroughly fed up with the fight. Pinder would not abandon the fight, but his hands might get sick of the discomfort.

Gathering a few sticks, I added them to the fire already laid, but under them I put a half dozen shotgun shells. In the tool shed were six sticks of powder and some fuse left from blasting rocks.

Digging out a crack at one corner of the fireplace, I put two sticks of dynamite into the crack, then ran the fuse within two inches of the fire and covered it with ashes. The shotgun shells would explode and scatter the fire, igniting, I hoped, the fuse.

A slow hour passed after I returned to a hideout in the brush. What was happening at the Two Bar? In any kind of fight, one has to have confidence in those fighting with him, and I had it in the men I'd left behind me. If one of them was killed, I vowed never to stop until all this crowd were finished.

Sweat trickled down my face. It was hot under the brush. Once a rattler crawled by within six or seven feet of me. A pack rat stared at me, then moved on. Crows quarreled in the trees over my head. And then I saw the riders.

One look told me. Whatever had happened at the Two Bar, I knew these men were not victorious. There were nine in the group, and two were bandaged. One had his arm in a sling, one had his skull bound up. Another man was tied over a saddle, head and heels hanging. They rode down the hill and I lifted my rifle, waiting for them to get closer to the ranch. Then I fired three times as rapidly as I could squeeze off the shots.

One horse sprang into the air, spun halfway around, scattering the group, then fell, sending his rider sprawling. The others rushed for the shelter of the buildings, but just as they reached them, one man toppled from his horse, hit the dirt like a sack of old clothes, and rolled over in the dust. He staggered to his feet and rushed toward the barn, fell again, then got up and ran on.

Others made a break for the house, and the first one to hit those greasy steps was Jim Pinder. He hit them running, his feet flew out from under him, and he hit the step on his chin. With a yell, the others charged by him, and even at that distance I could hear the crash of their falling, their angry shouts, and then the roaring sneezes and gasping yells as the red pepper filled the air and bit into their nostrils.

Coolly I proceeded to shoot out the windows, to knock the hinges off the door, and, when Jim Pinder staggered to his feet and reached for his hat, I put a bullet through the hat. He jumped as if stung and grabbed for his pistol. He swung it up, and I fired again as he did. What happened to his shot I never knew, but he dropped the pistol with a yell and plunged for the door.

One man had ducked for the heavily planked water trough and now he fired at me. Invisible from my position, I knew that he was somewhere under the trough, and so I drilled the trough with two quick shots, draining the water down upon him. He jumped to escape, and I put bullets into the dust to the left and right of his position. Like it or not, he had to lie there while all the water ran over him. A few scattered shots stampeded their horses, and then I settled down to wait for time to bring the real fireworks.

A few shots came my way after a while, but all were high or low and none came close to me.

Taking my time, I loaded up for the second time, and then rolled a smoke. My buckskin was in a low place and had cover from the shots. There was no way they could escape from the house to approach me. One wounded man had fallen near the barn, and I let him get up and limp toward it. Every once in a while, somebody would fall inside the house and in the clear air I could hear the sound and each time I couldn't help but grin.

There was smashing and banging inside the house, and I could imagine what was happening. They were looking for coffee and not finding it. A few minutes later a slow trickle of smoke came out the chimney. My head resting on the palm of one hand, I took a deep drag on my cigarette and waited happily for the explosions.

They came, and suddenly. There was the sharp bark of a shotgun shell exploding, then a series of bangs as the others went off. Two men rushed from the door and charged for the barn. Bullets into the dust hurried them to shelter, and I laid back and laughed heartily. I'd never felt so good in my life, picturing the faces of those tired, disgruntled men, besieged in the cabin, unable to make coffee, sliding on the greasy floor, sneezing from the red pepper, ducking shotgun shells from the fire.

Not five minutes had passed when the powder went off with terrific concussion. I had planted it better than I knew, for it not only cracked the fireplace but blew a hole in it from which smoke gulped, then trickled slowly.

Rising, I drifted back to my horse and headed for the ranch. Without doubt the CP outfit was beginning to learn what war meant, and, furthermore, I knew my methods were far more exasperating to the cowhands than out-and-out fight. Your true cowhand savors a good scrap, but he does not like discomfort or annoyance, and I knew that going without water, without good food, and without coffee would do more to end the fight than anything else. All the same, as I headed the gelding back toward the Two Bar, I knew that if any of my own boys had been killed, I would retaliate in kind. There could be no other answer.

Mulvaney greeted me at the door. "Sure, Matt, you missed a good scrap! We give them lads the fight of their lives!"

Jolly and Jonathan looked up at me. Jolly grinning, the more serious Jonathan smiling faintly. Jolly showed me a bullet burn on his arm, the only scratch any of them had suffered.

They had been watching, taking turnabout,

determined they would not be caught asleep while I was gone. The result was that they sighted the CP riders when they were still miles from the headquarters of the Two Bar. The Benaras boys began it with a skirmishers' battle, firing from rocks and brush in a continual running fight. A half dozen times they drove the CP riders to shelter, killing two horses and wounding a man.

They had retreated steadily until in a position to be covered by Mulvaney, who was ready with all the spare arms loaded. From the bunkhouse they stood off the attack. They had so many loaded weapons that there was no break in their fire until the CP retreated.

"Somebody didn't want to fight," Jolly explained. "We seen 'em argufyin' an' then finally somebody else joined in, an' they backed out on Pinder. He was almighty sore, believe you me."

Amid much laughter I told them about my own attack on the CP.

Mulvaney ended it suddenly. "Hey!" he turned swiftly. "I forgot to tell yer. That catamount of a Bodie Miller done shot Canaval!"

"Is he dead?"

"Not the last we heard, but he's hurt mighty bad. He took four bullets before he went down."

"Miller?"

"Never got a scratch. That kid's plumb poison, I tell you. Poison."

IX

For a minute I considered that, and liked none of it. Canaval had been a man with whom I could reason. More than that, with Canaval at hand there had always been protection for Olga.

There was no time to be wasted now. Telling Mulvaney of what I had seen in the cañon, I turned my buckskin toward the Bar M. I wanted first of all to talk with Olga, and second to see Canaval. If the man was alive, I had to talk to him. The gun star of Bodie Miller was rising now, and I knew how he would react. This new shooting would only serve to convince him of his speed. The confidence he had lacked on our first meeting he would now have.

He would not wait long to kill again, and he would seek out some known gunfighter, for his reputation could only grow now by killing the good ones, and Canaval had been one of the fastest around. And who would that mean? Jim Pinder, Morgan Park, or myself. And knowing how he felt about me, I had an idea who he would be seeking out.

Key Chapin was standing on the wide verandah of the Bar M house when I rode into the yard. Fox was loitering nearby and he started toward me.

"You ain't wanted here, Sabre," he told me brusquely. "Get off the place."

"Don't be a fool, man. I've come on business."

He shook his head stubbornly. "Don't make no diff'rence. Start movin' an' don't reach for a gun. You're covered from the bunkhouse an' the barn."

"Fox," I persisted, "I've no row with you, and you're the last man in the world I'd like to kill, but I don't like being pushed, and you're pushing me. I've got Bodie Miller and Morgan Park to take care of, as well as Jim Pinder. So get this straight. If you want to die, grab iron. Don't ride me, Fox, because I won't take it."

My buckskin started, and Fox, his face a study in conflicting emotion, hesitated. Then a cool voice interposed. "Fox! Step back! Let the gentleman come up."

It was Olga Maclaren.

Fox hesitated, then stepped back, and I drew up the buckskin for a minute. Fox looked up at me, and our eyes met.

"I'm glad of that, Fox," I said. "I'd hate to have killed a man as good as you. They don't come often."

The sincerity in my voice must have reached him, for when I happened to glance back, he was staring after me, his face puzzled. As I dismounted, Chapin walked over toward the house.

Olga stood on the steps, awaiting me. There was no welcome in her eyes. Her face was cool, composed. "There was something you wanted?"

"Is that my only welcome?"

"What reason have you to expect anything more?"

That made me shrug. "None," I said, "none at all. How's Canaval?"

"Resting."

"Is he better? Is he conscious?"

"Yes to both questions. Can he see anybody? No."

Then I heard him speak. "Sabre? Is that you? Come in!"

Olga hesitated, and for a minute I believed she was going to defy the request, then with a shrug of indifference she led Chapin and me into the wounded man's room.

The foreman's appearance shocked me. He was drawn and thin, his eyes huge and hollow in the deathly pallor of his face. His hand gripped mine and he stared up at me. "Glad you're here, Sabre," he said abruptly. "Watch that little demon. Oh, he's a fast man. He's blinding. He had a bullet into me before my gun cleared. He's a freak, Sabre."

"Sure," I agreed, "but that isn't what I came about. I came to tell you again. I had nothing to do with killing Rud Maclaren."

He nodded slightly. "I'm sure of it." I could

feel Olga behind me. "I found . . . tracks. Not yours. Horse tracks, and tracks of a man carrying a heavy burden. Small feet."

Chapin interrupted suddenly. "Sabre, I've a message for you. Picked it up in Silver Reef yesterday." He handed me a telegram, still sealed. Ripping it open, I saw there what I had expected.

MY BROTHER UNHEARD OF IN MANY MONTHS. MORGAN PARK ANSWERS DESCRIPTION OF PARK CANTWELL, WANTED FOR MURDER AND EMBEZZLEMENT OF REGI-MENTAL FUNDS. COMING WEST.

LEO D'ARCY
COL. 12TH CAVALRY

Without comment, I handed the message back to Chapin, who read it aloud. Olga grew pale, but she said nothing.

"Know anything about the case?" Canaval asked Chapin.

The editor nodded. "Yes, I do. It was quite an exciting case at the time. Park Cantwell was a captain in the cavalry. He embezzled some twenty thousand dollars, then murdered his commanding officer when faced with it. He got away, was recaptured, and then broke jail and killed two men in the process. He was last heard of in Mexico."

"Not much chance of a mistake, is there?"

"None," Chapin said, "or very slight. Not many men are so big, and he is a striking character. Out West here, he probably believed he would not be discovered. Most of his time he spent on that lonely ranch of his, and he rarely was around town until lately. Apparently, if this is true, he hoped to realize enough money out of this deal of his with Jake Booker to retire in Mexico or elsewhere. Probably in this remote corner of the West, he believed he might never be recognized."

"And now?" Olga asked. "What will happen?"

Chapin shrugged. "I'll take this message to Sheriff Will Tharp, and then we'll wait for D'Arcy to arrive."

"There's not much else we can do," I agreed.

"What is it Park and Booker want?" Chapin wondered. "I don't grasp their motive."

"Who does?" I shrugged.

Olga had not looked at me. Several times I tried to catch her eyes, but she avoided my glance. Her face was quiet, composed, and she was, as always, perfectly poised. Not by so much as a flicker of an eyelash did she betray her feelings toward me, but I found no comfort in that. Whether or not she believed I had killed her father, she obviously wanted no part of me. Discouraged, I turned toward the door.

"Where to now?" Canaval asked.

"Why"—I turned—"I'm heading for town to

see Morgan Park. No man ever beat me with his fists yet and walked away scotfree. I'll have the hide off that brute, and now is as good a time as any."

"Leave him alone. Sabre!" Canaval tried to sit up. "I've seen him kill a man with his fists!"

"He won't kill me."

"What is this?" Olga turned around, her eyes blazing. "A cheap childish desire for revenge? Or are you talking just to make noise? It seems all I've heard you do since you came here is to talk. You've no right to go in there and start trouble. You've no right to fight Morgan Park simply because he beat you. Leave him alone."

"Protecting him?" My voice was not pleasant. Did she, I wondered, actually love the man? The idea did not appeal to me, and the more it stayed in my mind the more angry I became.

"No!" she flared. "I am not protecting him! From what I saw of you after that first fight, I don't believe it is he who needs the protection."

She could have said nothing more likely to bring all my own temper to the surface. So, when she spoke, I listened, my face stiffening. Then without another word I turned and walked from the room. I went down the steps to my horse, and into the saddle.

The buckskin leaned into the wind and kept the fast pace I set for him. Despite my fury, I kept my eyes open and on the hills. Right then, I would have welcomed a fight and any kind of a fight. I was mad all the way through, burning with it.

And perhaps it was lucky that right then I should round a bend of the trail and come into the midst of a group of riders. They were heading the same way I was, toward town. They had not heard me until I rounded the bend, and then the sudden sound of my horse's hoof had turned their heads. One of the men called out: "Jack!" I knew then that I had come upon Jack Slade. And the devil dove for his gun.

He was too late. Mad clear through, the instant I saw them I slammed the spurs into my startled buckskin. The horse gave a lunge, driving between the last two riders and striking Slade's horse with his shoulder. At the same instant, I lashed out with the barrel of my Colt and laid it above the ear of the nearest rider. He went off his horse as if struck by lightning, and I swung around, blasting a shot from my belt that knocked the gun from the hand of another rider. Slade was fighting his maddened horse, and I leaned over and hit it a crack with my hat. The horse gave a tremendous leap and started to run like a scared rabbit with Slade fighting to stay in the saddle. He had lost one stirrup when my horse lunged into his and had not recovered it. The last I saw of him was his running horse and a cloud of dust. It all happened in a split second, and one man had a smashed hand, one was knocked out, and Slade was fighting his horse.

The fourth man had been maneuvering for a shot at me, but among the plunging horses he was afraid of hitting his own friends. Wheeling my horse, I fired as he did and both of us missed. He tried to steady his horse and swung. Buck did not like it and was fighting to get away. I let him go, taking a backward shot at the man in the saddle, a shot that must have clipped his ear for he ducked like a bee-stung farmer, and then Buck was laying them down on the trail to town.

Feeding shells into my gun, I let him run. I felt better for the action and was ready for anything. The town loomed up, and I rode in and swung down in front of Mother O'Hara's. Buck's side looked bad, for the spurs had bit deep, and I'm a man who rarely touches a spur to a horse. After greasing the wounds and talking Buck into friendship again, I went inside.

There was nobody around, but Katie O'Hara came out of her kitchen. One look at me and she could see I was spoiling for trouble.

"Morgan Park in town?"

She did not hesitate. "He is that. A moment ago I heard he was in the saloon."

Morgan Park was there, all right. He was sitting at a table with Jake Booker, and they both looked up when I entered. I didn't waste any time. I walked up to them.

"Booker," I said, "I've heard you're a no-account shyster, a sheep-stealing, small-town shyster, at that. But you're doing business with a thief and a murderer, and the man I'm going to whip." With that I grabbed the table and hurled it out of the way, and then I slapped Morgan Park across the mouth with my hat.

Morgan Park came off his chair with a roar. He lunged and came up fast, and I smashed him in the teeth with a left. His lips flattened and blood showered from his mouth, and then I threw a right that caught him flush on the chin—and I threw it hard!

He blinked, but he never stopped coming, and he rushed me, swinging with both of those huge, iron-like fists. One of them rang bells on my skull and the other dug for my mid-section with a blow I partially blocked with an elbow, then I turned with his arm over my shoulder, and I threw him bodily across the floor against the bar rail. He came up fast, and I nailed him with another left. Then he caught me with both hands, and sparks danced among the stars in my skull. That old smoky taste came up inside of me, and the taste of blood in my mouth, and I walked in smashing with both hands! Something busted on his face, and his brow was cut to the bone and the blood was running all over him.

There was a crowd around, and they were yelling, but I heard no sound. I walked in, bobbing and weaving to miss as many of those jarring, brutal blows as possible, but they kept landing and battering me. He knocked me back into the bar, and then grabbed a bottle. He took a terrific cut at my skull, and I ducked, smashing him in the ribs. He staggered and sprawled out of balance from the force of his missed swing, and I rushed him and took a flying leap at his shoulders. I landed astride and jammed both spurs into his thighs and he let out a roar of agony.

I went over his head, lighting on all fours, and he sprang atop my back. I flattened out on the floor with the feeling that he had me. He was yelling like a madman, and he grabbed my hair and began to beat my head against the floor. How I did it I'll never know, but I bowed my back under his weight and forced myself to my hands and knees. He ripped at me with his own spurs, and then I got his leg, and threw him off.

Coming up together, we circled, more wary now. His shirt was in ribbons, and he was covered with blood. I'd never seen Morgan stripped before. He had a chest and shoulders like a Hercules. He circled, and then came into me, snarling. I nailed that snarl into his teeth with both fists, and we stood there swinging freely with both hands, rocking with the power of those punches and smelling of sweat, blood, and fury.

He backed up, and I went into him. Suddenly he caught my upper arms and, dropping, put a foot in my stomach and threw me over his head! For a fleeting instant I was flying through the air, and then I lit on a poker table and grabbed the sides with both hands. It went over on top of me, and that was all that saved me as he rushed in to finish me with the boots. I shoved the table at him and came up off the floor, and he hit me again, and I went right back down. He dropped a big palm on my head and shoved me at the floor. I sprawled out and he kicked me in the side. It missed my ribs and glanced off my gun belt, and I rolled over and grabbed his boot, twisting hard.

It threw him off balance and he hit the floor, which gave me a chance to get on my feet. I got him just as he was halfway up with a right that knocked him through the door and out onto the porch. I hit the porch in a jump, and he tackled me around the knees. We both were down then, and I slapped him with a cupped hand over his ear and knew from the way he let go that I'd busted an eardrum for him. I dropped him again with a solid right to the chin, and stood back, gasping and pain-wracked, fighting for breath. He got up more slowly, and I nailed him, left and right in the mouth, and he went down heavily.

Sprawled out, he lay there on the edge of the walk, one hand trailing in the dust, and I stared down at him. He was finished—through! Turning on my heels, I walked back inside, and, brushing off those who crowded around me, I headed for the bar. I took the glass of whiskey that was shoved at me and poured it in my hands and mopped the cuts on the lower part of my face with it. Then I took a quick gulp from the glass that was again put before me, and turned.

Morgan Park was standing three feet away from me, a bloody, battered giant with cold, ugly fury blazing from his eyes. "Give me a drink!" he bellowed.

He picked up the glass and tossed it off. "Another!" he yelled, while I stared at him. He picked that up, lifted it to his lips, then threw it in my eyes!

I must have blinked, for instead of getting the shot glass full, I got only part of it, but enough to blind me. And then he stepped close. As I fought for sight, I caught a glimpse of his boot toes, wide spread, and I was amazed that such a big man had such small feet. Then he hit me. It felt like a blow from an axe, and it knocked me into the bar. He faced around, taking his time, and he smashed one into my body, and I went down, gasping for breath. He kicked at me with the toe of one of those deadly boots that could have put an eye out, but the kick glanced off the side of my head.

It was my turn to be down and out. Then somebody drenched me with a bucket of water, and I looked up. Key Chapin was standing over me, but it was not Key Chapin who had thrown the water. It was Olga.

Right then I was only amazed that she was there at all, and then I got up shakily and somebody said—"There he is!"—and I saw Park, standing there with his hands on his hips, leering at me, and with the same mutual hatred we went for each other again.

How we did it I don't know. Both of us had taken beatings that would have killed a horse. All I knew was that time for me had stopped. Only one thing remained. I had to whip that man, whip him or kill him with my bare hands, and I was not stopping until I was sure I had done it.

"Stop it, you crazy fools! Stop it or I'll throw you both in jail!" Sheriff Will Tharp was standing in the door with a gun on me. His cold blue eyes were blazing.

Behind him were maybe twenty men, staring at us. One of them was Key Chapin. Another was Bodie Miller.

"Take him out of here, then," I said. "If he wants more of this, he can have it in the morning."

Park backed toward the door, then turned away. He looked punch-drunk.

After that I sat up for an hour putting hot water on my face.

Then I went to the livery stable and crawled into the loft, taking a blanket with me. I had worn my guns and had my rifle along.

How long I slept I have no idea except that, when I awakened, bright sunlight was streaming through the cracks in the walls of the old stable, and the loft was like an oven with the heat. Sitting up, I touched my face. It was sore all right, but felt better. I worked my fingers to loosen them up, and then heard a movement and looked around. Morgan Park was on the ladder, staring at me. And I knew then that I was not looking at a sane man.

X

He stood there on the ladder in that hot old barn, staring at me with hatred and a fury that seemed no whit abated from the previous night.

"You back again?" I spoke quietly, yet lay poised for instant movement. I knew now the tremendous vitality that huge body held. "After the way I licked you last night?"

The veins distended in his brow and throat. "Whipped me?" His voice was hoarse with anger. "Why, you . . . !" He started over the end of the ladder, and I let him come. Right then I could have cooled him, knocked him off that ladder, but something within me wouldn't allow it. With a lesser man, one I could have whipped easily, I might have done it just to end the fighting, but not with Morgan Park. Right then I knew I had to whip him fairly, or I could never be quite comfortable again.

He straightened from the ladder, and I could see that he was a little stiff. Well, so was I. But my boxing with Mulvaney and the riding I had done had been keeping me trim. My condition was better than his, almost enough to equalize his greater size and strength. He straightened and turned toward me. He did not rush, just stood there studying me with cool calculation, and I knew that he, too, had come here to make an end to this fight and to me.

Right then he was studying how best to whip me, and suddenly I perceived his advantage. In the loft, one side open to the barn, the rest of it stacked with hay, I was distinctly at a disadvantage. Here his weight and strength could be decisive. He moved toward me, backing me toward the hay. I feinted, but he did not strike. He merely moved on in, his head hunched behind a big shoulder, his fists before him, moving slightly. Then he lunged. My back came up against the slanting wall of hay and my feet slipped. Off balance, lying against the hay, I had no power in my blows. With cold brutality he began to swing, his eyes were exultant and wicked with sadistic delight. Lights exploded in my brain, and then another punch hit me, and another.

My head spinning, my mouth tasting of smoke,

I let myself slide to a sitting position, then threw my weight sidewise against his knees. He staggered and, fearing the fall off the edge of the loft, fought for balance. Instantly I smashed him in the mouth. He went to his haunches, and I sprang past him, grabbed a rope that hung from the rafters and dropped to the hard-packed earth of the barn's floor.

He turned and glared at me, and I waited. A man appeared in the door, and I heard him yell: "They're at it again!" And then Morgan Park clambered down the ladder and turned to me.

Now it had to be ended. Moving in quickly, I jabbed a stiff left to his face. The punch landed on his lacerated mouth and started the blood. Circling carefully, I slipped a right, and countered with a right to the ribs. Then I hit him, fast and rolling my shoulders, with a left and right to the face. He came in, but I slipped another punch and uppercut hard to the wind. That slowed him down. He hit me with a glancing left and took two punches in return.

He looked sick now, and I moved in, smashing him on the chin with both hands. He backed up, bewildered, and I knocked his left aside and hit him on the chin. He went to his knees, and I stepped back and let him get up.

Behind me there was a crowd and I knew it. Waiting, I let him get up. He wiped off his hands, then lunged at me, head down and swinging.

Side-stepping swiftly, I evaded the rush, and, when he tried it again, I dropped my palm to the top of his head and spun him. At the same instant I uppercut with a wicked right that straightened him up. He turned toward me, and then I pulled the trigger on a high hard one. It struck his chin with the solid thud of the butt end of an axe striking a log.

He fell—not over backward, but face down. He lay there, still and quiet, unmoving. Out cold.

Sodden with weariness and fed up with fighting for once, I turned away from him and picked up my hat and rifle. Nobody said anything, staring at my battered face and torn clothing. Then they walked to him.

At the door I met Sheriff Tharp. He glared at me. "Didn't I tell you to stop fighting in this town, Sabre?"

"What am I going to do? Let him beat my head off? I came here to sleep without interruption and he followed me, found me this morning." Jerking my head toward the barn's interior, I told him: "You'll find him in there, Tharp."

He hesitated. "Better have some rest, Sabre. Then ride out of town for a few days. After all, I should have peace. I'm arresting Park."

"Not for fighting?"

"For murder. This morning I received an official communication confirming your message."

Actually, I was sorry for him. No man ever

hates a man he has whipped in a hand-to-hand fight. All I wanted now was sleep, food, and gallons of cold spring water. Right then I felt as if it had been weeks since I'd had a decent drink.

Yet all the way to O'Hara's I kept remembering that bucket of water doused over me the night before. Had it really been Olga Maclaren there? Or had I been out of my head from the punches I'd taken?

When my face was washed off, I came into the restaurant, and the first person I saw was Key Chapin. He looked at my face and shook his head. "I'd never believe anything human could fight the way you two did!" he exclaimed. "And again this morning! I hear you whipped him good this time."

"Yeah." I was tired of it all. Somberly I ate breakfast, listening to the drone of voices in my ears.

"Booker's still in town." Chapin was speaking. "What's he after, I wonder?"

Right then I did not care, but, as I ate and drank coffee, my mind began to function once more. After all, this was my country. I belonged here. For the first time, I really felt that I belonged some place.

"Am I crazy, or was Olga here last night?"

"She was here, all right. She saw part of your fight."

"Did she leave?"

"I think not. I believe she's staying over at Doc and Missus West's place. They're old friends of hers." Chapin knocked out his pipe. "As a matter of fact, you'd better go over there and have him look at those cuts. At least one of them needs some stitches."

"Tharp arrested Park."

"Yes, I know. Park is Cantwell, all right."

Out in the air I felt better. With food and some strong black coffee inside of me, I felt like a new man, and the mountain air was fresh and good to the taste. Turning, I started up the street, walking slowly. This was Hattan's Point. This was my town. Here, in this place, I would remain, I would ranch here, graze my cattle, rear my sons to manhood. Here I would take my place in the world and be something more than the careless, cheerful, trouble-hunting rider. Here, in this place, I belonged.

Doc West lived in a small white cottage surrounded by rose bushes and shrouded in vines. Several tall poplars reached toward the sky and there was a small patch of lawn inside the white picket fence.

He answered the door at my rap, a tall, austere-looking man with gray hair and keen blue eyes. He smiled at me. "You're Matt Sabre? I was expecting you."

That made me grin. "With a face like this, you should expect me. I took a licking for a while."

"And gave one to Morgan Park. I have just come from the jail where I looked him over. He has three broken ribs and his jaw is broken."

"No!" I stared at him.

He nodded. "The ribs were broken last night sometime, I'd guess."

"There was no quit in him."

West nodded seriously. "There still isn't. He's a dangerous man, Sabre. A very dangerous man."

That I knew. Looking around, I saw nothing of Olga Maclaren. Hesitating to ask, I waited and let him work on me. When he was finished, I got to my feet and buckled on my guns.

"And now?" he asked.

"Back to the Two Bar. There's work to do there."

He nodded, but seemed to be hesitating about something. Then he asked: "What about the murder of Rud Maclaren? What's your view on that?"

Something occurred to me then that I had forgotten. "It was Morgan Park," I said. "Canaval found the footprint of a man nearby. The boots were very small. Morgan Park . . . and I noticed it for the first time during our fight . . . has very small feet despite his size."

"You may be right," he agreed hesitantly. "I've wondered."

"Who else could it have been? I know I didn't do it."

"I don't believe you did, but . . . ," he hesitated, then dropped the subject.

Slowly I walked out to the porch and stopped there, fitting my hat on my head. It had to be done gently for I had two good-size lumps just at my hairline. A movement made me turn, and Olga was standing in the doorway.

Her dark hair was piled on her head, the first time I had seen it that way, and she was wearing something green and summery that made her eyes an even deeper green. For a long moment neither of us spoke, and then she said: "Your face . . . does it hurt very much?"

"Not much. It mostly just looks bad, and I'll probably not be able to shave for a while. How's Canaval?"

"He's much better. I've put Fox to running the ranch."

"He's a good man." I twisted my hat in my hands. "When are you going back?"

"Tomorrow, I believe."

How lovely she was! At this moment I knew that I had never in all my life seen anything so lovely, or anyone so desirable, or anyone who meant so much to me. It was strange, all of it. But how did she feel toward me?

"You're staying on the Two Bar?"

"Yes, my house is coming along now, and the cattle are doing well. I've started something there, and I think I'll stay. This," I said quietly, "is my home, this is my country. This is where I belong."

She looked up, and, as our eyes met, I thought she was going to speak, but she said nothing. Then I stepped quickly to her and took her hands. "Olga, you can't really believe that I killed your father? You can't believe I ever would do such a thing?"

"No. I never really believed you'd killed him."

"Then . . . ?"

She said nothing, not meeting my eyes.

"I want you, Olga. You, more than anything. I want you on the Two Bar. You are the reason I have stayed here, and you are the reason I am going to remain."

"Don't. Don't talk like that. We can never be anything to each other."

"What are you saying? You can't mean that."

"I do mean it. You . . . you're violent. You're a killer. You've killed men here, and I think you live for fighting. I watched you in that fight with Morgan. You . . . you actually enjoyed it."

Thinking that over, I had to agree. "In a way, yes. After all, fighting has been a necessity too long in the life of men upon earth. It is not an easy thing to be rid of. Mentally I know that violence is always a bad means to an end. I know that all disputes should be settled without it. Nevertheless, deep inside me, there is something

214

that does like it. It is too old a feeling to die out quickly, and as long as there are men in the world like Morgan Park, the Pinders, and Bodie Miller, there must be men willing and able to fight them."

"But why does it have to be you?" She looked up at me quickly. "Don't fight any more, Matt. Stay on the Two Bar for a while. Don't come to town. I don't want you to meet Bodie Miller. You mustn't. You mustn't!"

Shrugging, I drew back a little. "Honey, there are some things a man must do, some things he has to do. If meeting Bodie Miller is one of them, I'll do it. Meeting a man who challenges you may seem very foolish to a woman's world, but a man cannot live only among women. He must live with men, and that means he must be judged by their standards, and, if I back down for Miller, then I'm through here."

"You can go away. You could go to California. You could go and straighten out some business for me there. Matt, you could . . ."

"No. I'm staying here."

There were more words and hard words, but when I left her, I had not changed. Not that I underestimated Miller in any way. I had seen such men before. Billy the Kid had been like him. Bodie Miller was full of salt now. He was riding his luck with spurs. Remembering that sallow face with its hard, cruel eyes, I knew I could not live in the country around Hattan's Point without facing Miller.

Yet I saw nothing of Bodie Miller in Hattan's Point, and took the trail for the Two Bar, riding with caution. The chances were he was confident enough now to face me, especially after the smashing I'd taken. Moreover, the Slades were in the country and would be smarting over the beating I had given them.

The Two Bar looked better than anything I had seen in a long time. It was shadowed now with late evening, but the slow smoke lifted straight above the chimney, and I could see the horses in the corral. As I rode into the yard, a man materialized from the shadows. It was Jonathan Benaras, with his long rifle.

When I swung down from the saddle, he stared at my face, but said nothing. Knowing he would be curious, I explained simply. "Morgan Park and I had it out. It was quite a fight. He took a licking."

"If he looks worse'n you, he must be a sight."

"He does, believe me. Anybody been around?"

"Nary a soul. Jolly was down the wash this afternoon. Them cows are sure fattenin' up fast. You got you a mighty fine ranch here. Paw was over. He said, if you needed another hand, you could have Zeb for the askin'."

"Thanks. Your father's all man."

Jonathan nodded. "I reckon. We aim to be

neighbors to folks who'll neighbor with us. We won't have no truck with them as walks it high an' mighty. Paw took to you right off. Said you come an' faced him like a man an' laid your cards on the table."

Mulvaney grinned when I walked through the door, and then indicated the food on the table. "Set up. You're just in time."

It was good, sitting there in my own home, seeing the light reflecting from the dishes and feeling the warmth and pleasantness of it. But the girl I wanted to share these things with was not here to make it something more than just a house.

"You are silent tonight," Mulvaney said shrewdly. "Is it the girl, or is it the fight?"

I grinned and my face hurt with the grinning. "I was thinking of the girl, not of Park."

"I was wondering about the fight," Mulvaney said. "I wish I'd been there to see it."

I told them about it, and, as I talked, I began to wonder what Park would do now, for he would not rest easy in jail, and there was no telling what trick Jake Booker might be up to. And what was it they wanted? Until I knew that, I knew nothing,

The place to look was where the Bar M and the Two Bar joined. And tomorrow I would do my looking, and would do it carefully.

On this ride, Mulvaney joined me, and I welcomed the company as well as the Irishman's shrewd brain. We rode east, toward the vast wilderness that lay there, east toward the country where I had followed Morgan Park toward his rendezvous with Jack Slade. East, toward the maze of cañons, desert, and lonely lands beyond the river.

"See any tracks up that way before?" Mulvaney asked suddenly.

"Some," I admitted, "but I was following the fresh trail. We'll have a look around."

"Think it will be that silver you found out about in Booker's office?"

"Could be. We'll head for Dark Cañon Plateau and work north from there. I think that's the country."

"I'd feel better," Mulvaney admitted after a pause, "if we knew what had become of that Slade outfit. They'll be feelin' none too kindly after the whippin' you gave 'em."

I agreed. Studying the narrowing point, I knew we would soon strike a trail that led back to the northwest, a trail that would take us into the depths of Fable Cañon. Nearing that trail, I suddenly saw something that looked like a horse track. A bit later we found the trail of a single horse, freshly shod and heading northeast—a trail no more than a few hours old.

"Could be one o' the Slade outfit," Mulvaney speculated dubiously. "Park's in jail, an' nobody else would come over here."

We fell in behind, and I could see these tracks

must have been made during the night. At one place a hoof had slipped and the earth had not yet dried out. Obviously, then, the horse had passed after the sun went down.

We rode with increasing care, and we were gaining. When the cañon branched, we found a water hole where the rider had filled his canteen and prepared a meal. "He's no woodsman, Mulvaney. Much of the wood he used was not good burning wood and some of it green. Also, his fire was in a place where the slightest breeze would swirl smoke in his face."

"He didn't unsaddle," Mulvaney said, "which means he was in a hurry."

This was not one of Slade's outlaws, for always on the dodge nobody knew better than they how to live in the wilds. Furthermore, they knew these cañons. This might be a stranger drifting into the country, looking for a hide-out. But it was somewhere in this maze that we would find what it was that drew the interest of Morgan Park.

Scouting around, I suddenly looked up. "Mulvaney! He's whipped us! There's no trail out!"

"Sure 'n' he didn't take wings to get out of here," Mulvaney growled. "We've gone blind, that's what we've done."

Returning to the spring, we let the horses drink while I did some serious thinking. The rock walls offered no route of escape. The trail had been plain to this point, and then vanished. No tracks. He had watered his horse, prepared a meal—and afterward left no tracks. "It's uncanny," I said. "It looks like we've a ghost on our hands."

Mulvaney rubbed his grizzled jaw and chuckled. "Who would be better to cope with a ghost than a couple of Irishmen?"

"Make some coffee, you bog-trotter," I told him. "Maybe then we'll think better."

"It's a cinch he didn't fly," I said later, over coffee, "and not even a snake could get up these cliffs. So he rode in, and, if he left, he rode out."

"But he left no tracks, Matt. He could have brushed them out, but we saw no signs of brushing. Where does that leave us?"

"Maybe"—the idea came suddenly—"he tied something on his feet?"

"Let's look up the cañons. He'd be most careful right here, but if he is wearin' somethin' on his feet, the farther he goes, the more tired he'll be . . . or his horse will be."

"You take one cañon, and I'll take the other. We'll meet back here in an hour."

Walking, leading my buckskin, I scanned the ground. At no place was the sand hard-packed, and there were tracks of deer, lion, and an occasional bighorn. Then I found a place where wild horses had fed, and there something attracted me. Those horses had been frightened.

From quiet feeding they had taken off suddenly,

and no bear or lion would frighten them so. They would leave, but not so swiftly. Only one thing could make wild horses fly so quickly—man.

The tracks were comparatively fresh, and instinct told me this was the right way. The wild horses had continued to run. Where their tracks covered the bottom of the cañon, and where the unknown rider must follow them, I should find a clue. And I did, almost at once. Something foreign to the rock and manzanita caught my eye. Picking it free of a manzanita branch, I straightened up. It was sheep's wool.

Swearing softly, I swung into the saddle and turned back. The rider had brought sheepskins with him, tied pieces over his horse's hoofs and some over his own boots, and so left no defined tracks.

Mulvaney was waiting for me. "Find anything?"

He listened with interest, and then nodded. "It was a good idea he had. Well, we'll get him now."

The trail led northeast and finally to a high, windswept plateau unbroken by anything but a few towering rocks or low-growing sagebrush. We sat our horses, squinting against the distance, looking over the plateau and then out over the vast maze of cañons, a red, corrugated distance of land almost untrod by men.

"If he's out there," Mulvaney said, "we may

never find him. You could lose an army in that."

"We'll find him. My hunch is that it won't be far." I nodded at the distance. "He had no pack horse, only a canteen to carry water, and, even if he's uncommonly shrewd, he's not experienced in the wilds."

Mulvaney had been studying the country. "I prospected through here, boy." He indicated a line of low hills to the east. "Those are the Sweet Alice Hills. There are ruins ahead of us, and away yonder is Beef Basin."

"We'll go slow. My guess is we're not far behind him."

As if in acknowledgement of my comment, a rifle shot rang out sharply in the clear air! We heard no bullet, but only the shot, and then another, closer, sharper!

"He's not shootin' at us," Mulvaney said, staring with shielded eyes. "Where is he?"

"Let's move!" I called. "I don't like this spot!"

Recklessly we plunged down the steep trail into the cañon. Down, down, down. Racing around elbow turns of the switchback trail, eager only to get off the skyline and into shelter. If the unknown rider had not fired at us, who had he fired at? Who was the rider? Why was he shooting?

XI

Tired as my buckskin was, he seemed to grasp the need for getting under cover, and he rounded curves in that trail that made my hair stand on end. At the bottom we drew up in a thick cluster of trees and brush, listening. Even our horses felt the tension, for their ears were up, their eyes alert.

All was still. Some distance away a stone rattled. Sweat trickled behind my ear, and I smelled the hot aroma of dust and baked leaves. My palms grew sweaty and I dried them, but there was no sound. Careful to let my saddle creak as little as possible, I swung down, Winchester in hand. With a motion to wait, I moved away.

From the edge of the trees I could see no more than thirty yards in one direction, and no more than twenty in the other. Rock walls towered above and the cañon lay, hot and still, under the midday sun. From somewhere came the sound of trickling water, but there was no other sound or movement. My neck felt hot and sticky, my shirt clung to my shoulders. Shifting the rifle in my hands, I studied the rock walls with misgiving. Drying my hands on my jeans, I took a chance and moved out of my cover, moving to a narrow, six-inch band of shade against the far wall.

Easing myself to the bend of the rock, I peered around.

Sixty yards away stood a saddled horse, head hanging. My eyes searched and saw nothing, and then, just visible beyond a white, water-worn boulder, I saw a boot and part of a leg. Cautiously I advanced, wary for any trick, ready to shoot instantly. There was no sound but an occasional chuckle of water over rocks. Then suddenly I could see the dead man.

His skull was bloody, and he had been shot with a rifle and at fairly close range. He had probably never known what hit him. There was vague familiarity to him and his skull bore a swelling. This had been one of Slade's men who I had slugged on the trail to Hattan's Point.

The bullet had struck over the eye and ranged downward, which meant he had been shot from ambush, from a hiding place high on the cañon wall. Lining up the position, I located a tuft of green that might be a ledge.

Mulvaney was approaching me. "He wasn't the man we followed," he advised. "This one was comin' from the other way."

"He's one of the Slade crowd. Dry-gulched."

"Whoever he is," Mulvaney assured me, "we can't take chances. The fellow who killed this man shot for keeps."

We started on, but no longer were the tracks disguised. The man we followed was going more slowly now. Suddenly I spotted a boot print. "Mulvaney," I whispered hoarsely. "That's the track of the man who killed Rud Maclaren."

"But Morgan Park is in the hoosegow," Mulvaney protested.

"Unless he's broken out. But I'd swear that was the track found near Maclaren's body. The one Canaval found."

My buckskin's head came up and his nostrils dilated. Grabbing his nose, I stifled the neigh, then stared up the cañon. Less than a hundred yards away a dun horse was picketed near a patch of bunchgrass. Hiding our horses in a box cañon, we scaled the wall for a look around. From the top of the badly fractured mesa we could see all the surrounding country. Under the southern edge of the mesa was a cluster of ancient ruins, beyond them some deep cañons. With my glasses shielded from sun reflection by my hat, I watched a man emerge from a crack in the earth, carrying a heavy sack. Placing it on the ground, he removed his coat and with a pick and bar began working at a slab of rock.

"What's he doin'?" Mulvaney demanded, squinting his eyes.

"Prying a slab of rock," I told him, and, even as I spoke, the rock slid, rumbled with other débris, then settled in front of the crack. After a careful inspection, the man concealed his tools, picked up his sack and rifle, and started back.

Studying him, I could see he wore black jeans, very dusty now, and a small hat. His face was not visible. He bore no resemblance to anyone I had seen before. He disappeared near the base of the mountain and for a long time we heard nothing.

"He's gone," I said.

"We'd best be mighty careful," Mulvaney warned uneasily. "That's no man to be foolin' with, I'm thinkin'."

A shot shattered the clear, white radiance of the afternoon. One shot, and then another.

We stared at each other, amazed and puzzled. There was no other sound, no further shots. Then uneasily we began our descent of the mesa, sitting ducks if he was waiting for us. To the south and west the land shimmered with heat, looking like a vast and unbelievable city, long fallen to ruin. We slid into the cañon where we'd left the horses, and then the shots were explained.

Both horses were on the ground, sprawled in pools of their own blood. Our canteens had been emptied and smashed with stones. We were thirty miles from the nearest ranch, and the way lay through some of the most rugged country on earth.

"There's water in the cañons," Mulvaney said at last, "but no way to carry it. You think he knew who we were?"

"If he lives in this country, he knows that

buckskin of mine," I said bitterly. "He was the best horse I ever owned."

To have hunted for us and found us, the unknown man would have had to take a chance on being killed himself, but by this means he left us small hope of getting out alive.

"We'll have a look where he worked," I said. "No use leaving without knowing about that."

It took us all of an hour to get there, and night was near before we had dug enough behind the slab of rock to get at the secret. Mulvaney cut into the bank with his pick. Ripping out a chunk and grabbing it, he thrust it under my eyes, his own glowing with enthusiasm.

"Silver," he said hoarsely. "Look at it! If the vein is like that for any distance, this is the biggest strike I ever saw! Richer than Silver Reef!"

The ore glittered in his hand. There was what had killed Rud Maclaren and all the others. "It's rich," I said, "but I'd settle for the Two Bar."

Mulvaney agreed. "But still," he said, "the silver is a handsome sight."

"Pocket it, then," I said dryly, "for it's a long walk we have."

"But a walk we can do!" He grinned at me. "Shall we start now?"

"Tonight," I said, "when the walking will be cool."

We let the shadows grow long around us while

we walked and watched the thick blackness choke the cañons and deepen in the shadows of trees. We walked on steadily, with little talk, up Ruin Cañon and over a saddle of the Sweet Alice Hills, and down to the spring on the far side of the hills.

There we rested, and we drank several times. From the stars I could see that it had taken us better than two hours of walking to make less than five miles. But now the trail would be easier along Dark Cañon Plateau—and then I remembered Slade's camp. What if they were back there again? Holed up in the same place?

It was a thought, and to go down the cañon toward them was actually none out of the way. Although the walking might be rougher at times, we would have the stream beside us, a thing to be considered. Mulvaney agreed and we descended into the cañon.

Dark it was there, and quiet except for the rustle of water over stones, and there was a cool dampness that was good to our throats and skin after the heat. We walked on, taking our time, for we'd no records to break. And then we heard singing before we saw the reflection of the fire.

We walked on, moving more carefully, for the cañon walls caught and magnified every sound.

Three men were about the fire and one of them was Jack Slade. Two were talking while one man sang as he cleaned his rifle. We reached the edge of the firelight before they saw us, and I had my Winchester on them, and Mulvaney that cannon-like four-shot pistol of his.

"Grab the sky, Slade!" I barked the order at him, and his hand dropped, then froze.

"Who is it?" he demanded hoarsely, straining his eyes at us. Our faces being shielded by the brims of our hats, he could not see enough of them. I stepped nearer so the firelight reached under my hat brim.

"It's Matt Sabre," I said, "and I'm not wanting to kill you or anybody. We want two horses. You can lend them to us, or we'll take them. Our horses were shot by the same man that killed your partner."

Slade jerked, his eyes showing incredulity. "Killed? Lott killed?"

"That's right. Intentionally, or otherwise he met up with the *hombre* we were following. He drilled your man right over the eyes. We followed on, and he found where we left our horses and shot them both to leave us afoot."

"Damn a man that'll kill a horse," Slade said. "Who was he?"

"Don't know," I admitted. "Only he leaves a track like Morgan Park. At least, he's got a small foot."

"But Park's in jail," Mulvaney added.

"Not now he isn't," Slade said. "Morgan Park broke jail within an hour after darkness last night.

He pulled one of those iron bars right out of that old wall, stole a horse, and got away. He's on the loose and after somebody's scalp."

Park free! But the man we had followed had not been as big as Park was. I did not tell them that. "How about the horses?" I asked.

"You can have them, Sabre," Slade said grudgingly. "I'm clearing out. I've no stomach for this sort of thing."

"Are they spares?"

Slade nodded. "We've a half dozen extras. In our business it pays to keep fresh horses." He grinned. "No hard feelin's, Sabre?"

"Not me," I said. "Only don't you boys get any wild ideas about jumping me. My trigger finger is right jittery."

Slade shrugged wryly. "With two guns on us? Not likely. I don't know whether your partner can shoot or not, but, with a cannon that big, he doesn't need to. What kind of a gun is that, anyway?"

"She's my own make," Mulvaney said cheerfully, "but the slug kills just as dead."

"Give this *hombre* an old stove pipe and he'd make a cannon," I told them. "He's a genius with tools."

While Mulvaney got the horses, I stood over the camp. "Any other news in town?" I asked Slade.

"Plenty," he admitted. "Some Army officer

230

came into town claimin' Park killed his brother. Seems a right salty gent. And"—his eyes flickered to mine—"Bodie Miller is talkin' it big around town. He says you're his meat."

"He's a heavy eater, that boy," I said carelessly. "He may tackle something one of these days that will give him indigestion."

Jack Slade shrugged and watched Mulvaney lead up the horses. As we mounted, I glanced back at him. "We'll leave these horses at the corral of the livery stable in town, if you like."

Slade's eyes twinkled a little. "Better not. First time you get a chance take 'em to a corral you'll find in the woods back of Armstrong's. Towns don't set well with me, nor me with them."

The horses were fresh and ready to go, and we let them run.

Daylight found us riding up the street of Hattan's Point, a town that was silent and waiting. The loft was full of hay and both of us headed for it. Two hours later I was wide awake. Splashing water on my face, I headed for O'Hara's. The first person I saw as we came through the door was Key Chapin. Olga Maclaren was with him.

Chapin looked up as we entered. "Sorry, Sabre," he said. "I've just heard."

"Heard what?" I was puzzled.

"That you're losing the Two Bar."

"Are you crazy? What are you talking about?"

"You mean you haven't heard? Jake Booker

showed up the other day and filed a deed to the Two Bar. He purchased the rights to it from Ball's nephew, the legitimate heir. He also has laid claim to the Bar M, maintaining that it was never actually owned by Rud Maclaren, but belonged to his brother-in-law, now dead. Booker has found some relative of the brother-in-law's and bought his right to the property."

"Well of all the . . . that's too flimsy, Chapin. He can't hope to get away with that! What's on his mind?"

Chapin shrugged. "If he goes to court, he can make it tough. You have witnesses to the fact that Ball gave you the ranch, but whether that will stand in court, I don't know. Especially with a shrewd operator like Booker fighting it. As to Maclaren, it turns out he did leave the ranch to his brother-in-law during a time some years ago when he was suffering from a gunshot wound, and apparently he never made another will. What's important right now is that Jake is going to court to get both you and Olga off the ranches and he plans to freeze all sales, bank accounts, and other money or stock until the case is settled."

"In other words, he doesn't want us to have the money to fight him."

Chapin shrugged. "I don't know what his idea is, but I'll tell you one thing. He stands in well with the judge, who is just about as crooked as he is, and they'll use your reputation against you. Don't think Booker hasn't considered all the angles, and don't think he doesn't know how flimsy his case may be. He'll bolster it every way possible, and he knows every trick in the book."

I sat down. This had come so suddenly that it took the wind out of my sails. "Has this news gone to the Bar M yet? Has it got out to Canaval?"

Chapin shrugged. "Why should it? He was only the foreman. Olga has been told and you can imagine how she feels."

My eyes went to hers, and she looked away. Katie O'Hara came in, and I gave her my order for breakfast and tried the coffee she had brought with her. It tasted good.

Sitting there, my mind began to work swiftly. There was still a chance, if I figured things right. Jake Booker was no fool. He had not paid out money for those claims unless he believed he could make them stand in court. He knew about how much money I had, and knew that Olga Maclaren, with the ranch bank accounts frozen, would be broke. Neither of us could afford to hire an attorney, and so far as that went there was no attorney within miles able to cope with Booker. What had started as a range war had degenerated into a range steal by a shyster lawyer, and he had arguments that could not be answered with a gun.

"How was Canaval when you left?"

"Better," Olga said, still refusing to meet my eyes.

"What about Morgan Park? I heard he escaped."

"Tharp's out after him now. That Colonel D'Arcy went with him and the posse. There had been a horse left for Park. Who was responsible for that, we don't know, but it may have been one of his own men."

"Where did Tharp go?"

"Toward the ranch, I think. There was no trail they could find."

"They should have gone east, toward Dark Cañon. That's where he'll be."

Chapin looked at me curiously, intently. "Why there?"

"That's where he'll go," I replied definitely. "Take my word for it."

They talked a little between them, but I ate in silence, always conscious of the girl across the table, aware of her every move.

Finishing my meal, I got up and reached for my hat. Olga looked up quickly. "Don't go out there. Bodie Miller is in town."

"Thanks." Our eyes met and held. Were they saying something to me? Or was I reading into their depths the meaning I wanted them to hold? "Thanks," I repeated. "I'd prefer not to meet him now. This is no time for personal grudges."

It was a horse I wanted, a better horse than

the one borrowed from Slade, and which might have been stolen. This, I reflected dryly, would be a poor time to be hanged as a horse thief. There was no gate at the corral on this side, so I climbed over, crossing the corral. At the corner I stopped in my tracks. A horse was tied to the corral, a horse stripped but recently of a saddle, a dun horse that showed evidence of hard riding. And in the damp earth near the trough was a boot print. Kneeling, I examined the hocks of the tied horse. From one of them I picked a shred of wool, then another. Spinning around, I raced for the restaurant. "Katie!" I demanded. "Who owns that horse? Did you see the rider?"

"If you're thinkin' o' Park, that horse couldn't carry him far. An' he would not stay in the town. Not him."

"Did you see anyone else?"

"Nobody . . . wait a minute! I did so. 'Twas Jake Booker. Not that I saw him with the horse, but a bit before daylight he came around the corner from that way and asked if I'd coffee ready."

Booker! He had small feet. He was in with Park. He wanted Maclaren dead. He had killed Slade's man and shot our horses. Booker had some explaining to do.

Mulvaney was crawling from the loft where I'd slept but was attentive at once. He listened, then ran to the stable office. Waiting only until he was on a horse and racing from town to the ranch, I started back to O'Hara's. My mind was made up.

The time had come for a showdown, and this time we would all be in it, and Jake Booker would not be forgotten.

Key Chapin looked up when I came in. "Key," I said quickly, "this is the pay-off. Find out for me where Booker is. Get somebody to keep an eye on him. He's not to leave town if he tries. Keep him under observation all the time until Mulvaney gets back from the ranch." Turning to Olga, I asked her: "How about Canaval? Can he ride yet? Could he stand a buckboard trip?"

She hesitated. "He couldn't ride, but he might stand it in the buckboard."

"Then get him into town, and have the boys come with him. Fox especially. I like that man Fox, and Canaval may need protection. Bring him in, and bring him here."

"What is it? What have you learned?" Chapin demanded.

"About everything I need to know," I replied. "We're going to save the Bar M for Olga, and perhaps we'll save my ranch, too. In any event, we'll have the man who killed Rud Maclaren!"

"What?" Olga's face was pale. "Matt, do you mean that?"

"I do. I only hope that Tharp gets back with Morgan Park, but I doubt if we'll see him again." Turning to Key, who was at the door. "Another thing. We might as well settle it all. Send a rider to the CP and have Jim Pinder get here. Get him here fast. We'll have our showdown the first thing in the morning."

Twice I walked up the street and back. Nowhere was there any sign of Bodie Miller, or of Red, his riding partner. The town still had that sense of expectancy that I had noticed upon riding in. And they were right—for a lot of things were going to happen and happen fast.

Key met me in the saloon. He walked toward me quickly, his face alive with interest. "What have you got in mind, Matt? What are you planning?"

"Several things. In the first place, there has been enough fighting and trouble. We're going to end it right here. We're going to close up this whole range fight. There aren't going to be any halfway measures. How well do you know Tharp?"

"Very well, why?"

"Will he throw his weight with us? It would mean a lot if he would."

"You can bank on him. He's a solid man, Matt. Very solid."

"All right, in the morning then. In the morning we'll settle everything."

There was a slight movement at the door and I looked up. My pulse almost stopped with the shock of it.

Bodie Miller stood there, his hands on his hips, his lips smiling. "Why, sure!" he said. "If that's what you want. The morning is as good a time as any."

XII

The sun came up, clear and hot. Already at daybreak the sky was without a cloud, and the distant mountains seemed to shimmer in a haze of their own making. The desert lost itself in heat waves before the day had scarce begun, and there was a stillness lying upon both desert and town, a sort of poised awareness without sound.

When I emerged upon the street, I was alone. Like a town of ghosts, the street was empty, silent except for the echo of my steps on the boardwalk. Then, as if their sound had broken the spell, the saloon door opened and the bartender emerged and began to sweep off the walk. He glanced quickly around at me, bobbed his head, and then with an uneasy look finished his sweeping hurriedly and ducked back inside. A man carrying two wooden buckets emerged from an alley and looked cautiously about. Assured there was no one in sight, he started across the street, glancing apprehensively first in one direction, then the other.

Sitting down in one of the polished chairs

238

before the saloon, I tipped back my hat and stared at the mountains. In a few minutes or a few hours, I might be dead.

It was not a good morning on which to die—but what morning is? Yet in a few minutes or hours another man and myself would probably meet out there in that street, and we would exchange shots, and one or both of us would die.

A rider came into the street. Mulvaney. He left his horse at the stable and clumped over to me. He was carrying enough guns to fight a war.

"They're comin'," Mulvaney said, "the whole kit an' caboodle of 'em. Be here within the hour. Jolly's already in town. Jonathan went after the others."

Nodding, I watched a woman looking down the street from the second floor. Suddenly she turned and left the window as if she had seen something or been called.

"Eat yet?"

"Not yet."

"Seen Olga? Or Chapin?"

"No."

"If Red cuts into this scrap," Mulvaney said, "he's mine."

"You can have him."

A door slammed somewhere, and then the man with the two wooden buckets hurried fearfully across the street, slopping water at every step.

"All right," I said, "we'll go eat."

There was no sign of Bodie Miller, or of Jim Pinder. Sheriff Tharp was still out hunting Morgan Park. Unless he got back soon, I'd have to run my show alone.

Mother O'Hara had a white tablecloth over the oilcloth, and her best dishes were out. She brought me coffee and said severely: "You should be ashamed. That girl laid awake half the night, thinkin' of nothin' but you!"

"About me?" I was incredulous.

"Yes, about you! Worried fair sick, she is! About you an' that Bodie Miller!"

The door opened and Olga walked in. Her eyes were very green today, and her hair drawn back in a loose knot at the back of her neck, but curled slightly into two waves on her forehead. She avoided my glance, and it was well she did, or I'd have come right out of my chair.

Then men entered the restaurant—Chapin, looking unusually severe, Colonel D'Arcy, and, last of all, Jake Booker.

D'Arcy caught my eye and a slow smile started on his lips. "Sabre! Well, I'm damned! The last time I saw Sabre he was in China!"

He took my hand and we grinned at each other. He was much older than I, but we talked the same language. His hair was gray at the temples.

"They say you've had trouble with Cantwell."

"And more to come if the sheriff doesn't get him. Park is mixed up in a shady deal with Jake

Booker, the man across the table from me."

"I?" Booker smiled but his eyes were deadly. "You're mistaken, Mister Sabre. It is true that Mister Park asked me to represent him in some trouble he was having, but we've no other connection. None at all."

Jim Pinder stalked in at that moment, but, knowing that Mulvaney and Jolly were watching, I ignored him.

"From the conversation I overheard in Silver Reef," I said to Booker, "I gathered you had obtained a buyer for some mining property he expected to have."

Fury flickered across his face. He had no idea how much I knew.

"It might interest you to know, Booker, that the fighting in this area is over. Pinder is here and we're having a peace meeting. Pinder is making a deal with us and with the Bar M. The fun's over."

"I ain't said nothin' about no deal," Pinder declared harshly. "I come in because I figured you was ready to sell."

"I might buy, Pinder, but I wouldn't sell. Furthermore, I'm with Chapin and Tharp in organizing this peace move. You can join or stay out, but if you don't join, you'll have to haul supplies from Silver Reef. This town will be closed to you. Each of us who has been in this fight is to put up a bond to keep the peace, effective at daybreak tomorrow. You can join or leave the country."

"After you killed my brother?" Pinder demanded. "You ask for peace?"

"You started the trouble in the livery stable, figuring you were tough enough to hire me or run me out of the country. You weren't big enough or fast enough then, and you aren't now. Nobody doubts your nerve. You've too much for your own good, and so have the lot of us, but it gets us nothing but killing and more killing. You can make money on the CP, or you can try to buck the country. As for Rollie, he laid for me and he got what he asked for. You're a hard man, Pinder, but you're no fool, and I've an idea you're square. Isn't it true Rollie started out to get me?"

Pinder hesitated, rubbing his angular jaw. "It is," he said finally, "but that don't make no . . ."

"It makes a lot of difference," I replied shortly. "Now look, Pinder. You've lost more than you've cost us. You need money. You can't ship cattle. You sign up or you'll never ship any. Everybody here knows you've nerve enough to face me, but everybody knows you'd die. All you'd prove would be that you're crazy. You know I'm the faster man."

He stared stubbornly at the table. Finally, he said: "I'll think it over. It'll take some time."

"It'll take you just two minutes," I said, laying it on the line.

He stared hard at me, his knuckles whitening on the arms of the chair. Suddenly, reluctantly he grinned. Sinking back into his chair, he shrugged. "You ride a man hard, Sabre. All right, peace it is."

"Thanks, Pinder." I thrust out my hand.

He hesitated, then took it. Katie O'Hara filled his cup.

"Look," he said, "I've got to make a drive. The only way there's water is across your place."

"What's wrong with that? Drive 'em across, and whatever water your herd needs is yours. Just so it doesn't take you more than a week to get 'em across."

Pinder smiled bleakly, but with humor. "Aw, you know it won't take more'n a day." He subsided into his chair and started on the coffee.

Jake Booker had been taking it all in, looking from one to the other of us with his sharp little eyes.

Canaval opened the door and stepped in, looking pale and drawn, followed by Tom Fox. "Miss Olga could have signed for me," he said. "She's the owner."

"You sign, too," I insisted. "We want to cover every eventuality."

Booker was smiling. He rubbed his lips with his thin, dry fingers. "All nonsense," he said briskly. "Both the Bar M and the Two Bar belong to me. I've filed the papers. You've twenty-four hours to get off and stay off."

"Booker," I said, "has assumed we are fools. He believed, if he could get a flimsy claim, he could get us into court and beat us. Well, this case will never go to court."

Booker's eyes were beady. "Are you threatening me?"

Sheriff Will Tharp came into the room. His eyes rested on Jake but he said nothing.

"We aren't threatening," I said. "On what does your claim to the Bar M stand?"

"Bill of sale," he replied promptly. "The ranch was actually left to Jay Collins, the gunfighter. He was Maclaren's brother-in-law. His will left all his property to a nephew, and I bought it, including the Bar M and all appurtenances thereto."

Canaval gave me a brief nod. "Sorry, Jake. You've lost your money. Jay Collins is not dead."

The lawyer jumped as if slapped. "Not dead? I saw his grave!"

"Booker"—I smiled—"look down the table at Jay Collins." I pointed to Canaval.

Booker broke into a fever of protest, but I was looking at Olga Maclaren. She was staring at Canaval, and he was smiling.

"Sure, honey," he said. "That's why I knew so much about your mother. She was the only person in the world I ever really loved . . . until I knew my niece."

Booker was worried now, really worried. In

a matter of minutes half his plan had come to nothing. He was shrewd enough to know we would not bluff, and that we had proof of what we said.

"As for the Two Bar," I added, "don't worry about it. I've my witnesses that the estate was given me. Not that it will matter to you."

"What's that? What'd you mean?" Booker stared at me.

"Because you were too greedy. You'll never rob another man, Booker. For murder, you'll hang."

He protested, but now he was cornered and frightened.

"You killed Rud Maclaren," I told him, "and, if that's not enough, you killed one of Slade's men from ambush. We can trail your horse to the scene of the crime, and, if you think a Western jury won't take the word of an Indian tracker, you're wrong."

"*He* killed Maclaren?" Canaval asked incredulously.

"He got him out of the house on some trumped-up excuse. To show him the silver, or to show him something I was planning . . . it doesn't matter what excuse was used. He shot him, then loaded him on a horse and brought him to my place. He shot him again, hoping to draw me to the vicinity as he wanted my tracks around the body."

"Lies!" Booker was recovering his assurance.

"Sabre had trouble with Maclaren, not I. We knew each other only by sight. The idea that I killed him is preposterous." He got to his feet. "In any event, what have the ranches to do with the silver claim of which you speak?"

"Morgan Park found the claim while trailing a man he meant to murder, Arnold D'Arcy, who knew him as Cantwell. Arnold had stumbled upon the old mine. Park murdered him only to find there was a catch in the deal. D'Arcy had already filed on the claim and had done assessment work on it. Legally, there was no way Park could gain possession, and no one legally could work the mine until D'Arcy's claim lapsed. Above all, Park wanted to avoid any public connection with the name of D'Arcy. He couldn't sell the claim, because it wasn't his, but if he could get control of the Bar M and the Two Bar, across which anyone working the claim must go, he could sell them at a fabulous price to an unscrupulous buyer. The new owner of the ranches could work the claim quietly, and by owning the ranches he could deny access to the vicinity so it would never be discovered what claims were being worked. When D'Arcy's assessment work lapsed, the claims could be filed upon by the new owners."

"Booker was to find a buyer?" asked Tharp.

"Yes. Park wanted money, not a mine or a ranch. Booker, I believe, planned to be that buyer himself. ~~He wanted~~ possession of the Bar M, so he decided to murder Rud Maclaren."

"You've no case against me that would stand in court!" Booker sneered. "You can prove nothing! What witnesses do you have?"

We had none, of course. Our evidence was a footprint. All the rest of what I'd said was guesswork. Tharp couldn't arrest the man on such slim grounds. We needed a confession.

Tom Fox leaned over the table, his eyes cold. "Some of us are satisfied. We don't need witnesses an' we don't need to hear no more. Some of us are almighty sure you killed Rud Maclaren. Got any arguments that will answer a six-gun? Or a rope?"

Booker's face thinned down and he crouched back against his chair. "You can't do that! The law! Tharp will protect me!"

Sighting a way clear, I smiled. "That might be, Booker. Confess, and Tharp will protect you. He'll save you for the law to handle. But if you leave here a free man, you'll be on your own."

"An' I'll come after you," Fox said.

"Confess, Booker." I suggested, "and you'll be safe."

"Aw! Turn him loose!" Fox protested angrily. "No need to have trouble, a trial an' all. Turn him loose! We all know he's a crook an' we all know he killed Rud Maclaren! Turn him loose!"

Booker's eyes were haunted with fear. There

was no acting in Tom Fox and he knew it. The rest of us might bluff, but not Fox. The Bar M hand wanted to kill him, and, given an opportunity, he would.

Right then I knew we were going to win. Jake Booker was a plotter and a conniver, not a courageous man. His mean little eyes darted from Fox to the sheriff. His mouth twitched and his face was wet with sweat. Tom Fox, his hand on his gun, moved relentlessly closer to Booker.

"All right, then!" he screamed. "I did it! I killed Maclaren. Now, Sheriff, save me from this man!"

I relaxed at last, as Tharp put the handcuffs on Booker. As they were leaving, I said: "What about Park? What happened to him?"

Tharp cleared his throat. "Morgan Park is dead. He was killed last night on the Woodenshoe."

We all looked at him, waiting. "That Apache of Pinder's killed him," Tharp explained. "Park ran for it after he busted out of jail. He killed his horse crossin' the flats an' he run into the Injun with a fresh horse. He wanted to swap, the 'Pache wouldn't go for the deal, so Park tried to dry-gulch him. He should have knowed better. The Injun killed him an' lit out."

"You're positive?" D'Arcy demanded.

Tharp nodded. "Yeah, he died hard, Park did."

The door opened and Jonathan Benaras was standing there. "Been scoutin' around," he said.

"Bodie Miller's done took out. He hit the saddle about a half hour back an' headed north out of town."

Bodie Miller gone! It was impossible. Yet, he had done it. Miller was gone! I got to my feet. "Good," I said quietly, "I was afraid there would be trouble."

Pinder got to his feet. "Don't you trust that Miller," he said grudgingly. "He's a snake in the grass. You watch out."

So, there it was. Pinder was no longer an enemy. The fight had been ended and I could go back to the Two Bar. I should feel relieved, and yet I did not. Probably it was because I had built myself up for Bodie Miller and nothing had come of it. I was so ready, and then it all petered out to nothing at all.

Olga had the Bar M, and her uncle to run it for her, and nobody would be making any trouble for Canaval. There was nothing for me to do but to go back home.

My horse was standing at the rail and I walked out to him and lifted the stirrup leather to tighten the cinch. But I did not hurry. Olga was standing there in front of the restaurant, and the one thing I wanted most was to talk to her. When I looked up, she was standing there alone.

"You're going back to the Two Bar?" Her voice was hesitant.

"Where else? After all, it's my home now."

"Have . . . have you done much to the house yet?"

"Some." I tightened the cinch, then unfastened the bridle reins. "Even a killer has to have a home." It was rough, and I meant it that way.

She flushed. "You're not holding that against me?"

"What else can I do? You said what you thought, didn't you?"

She stood there, looking at me, uncertain of what to say, and I let her stand there.

She watched me put my foot in the stirrup and swing into the saddle. She looked as if she wanted to say something, but she did not. Yet, when I looked down at her, she was more like a little girl who had been spanked than anything else I could think of.

Suddenly I was doing the talking. "Ever start that trousseau I mentioned?"

She looked up quickly. "Yes," she admitted, "but . . . but I'm afraid I didn't get very far with it. You see, there was . . ."

"Forget it." I was brusque. "We'll do without it. I was going to ride out of here and let you stay, but I'll be double damned if I will. I told you I was going to marry you, and I am. Now, listen, trousseau or not, you be ready by tomorrow noon, understand?"

"Yes. All right. I mean . . . I will."

Suddenly we were both laughing like fools and

I was off that horse and kissing her, and all the town of Hattan's Point could see us. It was right there in front of the café, and I could see people coming from the saloons and standing along the boardwalks, all grinning.

Then I let go of her and stepped back, and said: "Tomorrow noon. I'll meet you here." And with that I wheeled my horse and lit out for the ranch.

Ever feel so good it looks as if the whole world is your big apple? That was the way I felt. I had all I ever wanted. Grass, water, cattle, and with a home and wife of my own. The trail back to the Two Bar swung around a huge mesa and opened out on a wide desert flat, and far beyond it I could see the suggestion of the stones and pinnacles of badlands beyond Dry Mesa. A rabbit burst from the brush and sprinted off across the sage, and then the road dipped down into a hollow. There, in the middle of the road, was Bodie Miller.

He was standing with his hands on his hips, laughing, and there was a devil in his eyes. Off to one side of the road was Red, holding their horses and grinning, too.

"Too bad!" Bodie said. "Too bad to cut down the big man just when he's ridin' highest, but I'll enjoy it."

This horse I rode was skittish and unacquainted with me. I'd no idea how he'd stand for shooting, and I wanted on the ground. Suddenly I slapped spurs to that gelding, and, when the startled animal lunged toward the gunman, I went off the other side. Hitting the ground running, I spun on one heel and saw Bodie's hands blur as they dove for their guns, and then I felt my own gun buck in my hand. Our bullets crossed each other, but mine was a fraction the fastest despite that instant of hesitation when I made sure it would count.

His slug ripped a furrow across my shoulder that stung like a thousand needles, but my own bullet caught him in the chest and he staggered back, his eyes wide and agonized. Then I started forward and suddenly the devil was up in me. I was mad, mad as I had never been before. I opened up with both guns. "What's the matter?" I was yelling. "Don't you like it, gunslick? You asked for it, now come and get it! Fast, are you? Why you cheap, two-bit gunman, I'll . . . !"

But he was finished. He stood there, a slighter man than I was, with blood turning his shirt front crimson, and with his mouth ripped by another bullet. He was white as death, even his lips were gray, and against that whiteness was the splash of blood. In his eyes now there was another look. The killing lust was gone, and in its place was an awful terror, for Bodie Miller had killed, and enjoyed it with a kind of sadistic bitterness that was in him—but now he knew he was being killed and the horror of death was surging through him.

"Now you know how they felt, Bodie," I said

bitterly. "It's an ugly thing to die with a slug in you because some punk wants to prove he's tough. And you aren't tough, Bodie, just mean."

He stared at me, but he didn't say anything. He was gone, and I could see it. Something kept him upright, standing in that white-hot sun, staring at me, the last face he would ever look upon.

"You asked for it, Bodie, but I'm sorry for it. Why didn't you stay to punching cows?"

Bodie backed up another step, and his gun slid from his fingers. He tried to speak, and then his knees buckled, and he went down. Standing over him, I looked at Red.

"I'm ridin'," Red said huskily. "Just give me a chance." He swung into the saddle, then looked down at Bodie. "He wasn't so tough, was he?"

"Nobody is," I told him. "Nobody's tough with a slug in his belly."

He rode off, and I stood there in the trail with Bodie dead at my feet. Slowly I holstered my guns, then led my horse off the trail to the shade where Bodie's horse still stood.

Lying there in the dusty trail, Bodie Miller no longer looked mean or even tough, he looked like a kid that had tackled a job that was too big for him.

There was a small gully off the trail. It looked like a grave, and I used it that way. Rolling him into it, I shoved the banks in on top of him, and then piled on some stones. Then I made a cross for him and wrote his name on it, and the words: HE PLAYED OUT HIS HAND. Then I hung his guns on the cross along with his hat.

It was not much of an end for a man, not any way you looked at it, but I wanted no more reputation as a killer—mine had already grown too big.

Maybe Red would tell the story, and maybe in time somebody would see the grave, but if Red's story was told, it would be somewhere far away and long after, and that suited me.

A stinging in my own shoulder reminded me of my own wound, but when I opened my shirt and checked my shoulder, I found it a mere scratch.

Ahead of me the serrated ridges of the wild lands were stark and lonely along the sky, and the sun behind me was picking out the very tips of the peaks to touch them with gold. Somehow the afternoon was gone, and now I was riding home to my own ranch, and tomorrow was my wedding day.

Books are produced in the United States using U.S.-based materials

Books are printed using a revolutionary new process called THINKtech™ that lowers energy usage by 70% and increases overall quality

Books are durable and flexible because of smythe-sewing

Paper is sourced using environmentally responsible foresting methods and the paper is acid-free

Center Point Large Print
600 Brooks Road / PO Box 1
Thorndike, ME 04986-0001 USA

(207) 568-3717

US & Canada:
1 800 929-9108
www.centerpointlargeprint.com